DRAGGED
FROM UNDER

THE BULL SHARK

DRAGGED FROM UNDER

DRAGGED FROM UNDER

THE BULL SHARK

Joseph Monninger

Scholastic Inc.

Text copyright © 2020 by Joseph Monninger
Photos © Shutterstock: cover font and throughout (zphoto), i–iii (solarseven), 56, 78 (Sloth Astronaut).

ISBN 978-1-338-58766-1

10 9 8 7 6 5 4 3 2 1   20 21 22 23 24

Printed in the U.S.A.   40
First printing 2020

Book design by Stephanie Yang

For Susan

**The cure for anything is salt water;
sweat, tears or the sea.**

—Isak Dinesen

**Fishes live in the sea, as men do a-land;
the great ones eat up the little ones.**

—William Shakespeare

PROLOGUE

First Attack

Robby White ran as hard as he could toward the canal. When he hit the last board of the dock, he pushed off into the air and tucked his knees into his chest. He was a good athlete, a junior forward on his New Jersey high school basketball team, and he tried to get as much air as he could. He let out a yelp when he reached the top of his jump, then he closed his eyes and readied for contact with the water.

Swackakk, he splashed into the canal.

He knifed down seven or eight feet, then spread his arms and legs and swam back to the surface. As soon as his head cleared the water, he yelled again. This time he called to his buddy, Jason St. John, to get in.

1

"It's amazing!" he called. "Hot, but good. What are you waiting for, you bonehead?"

"It's Florida, you butt. Of course it's warm!" Jason yelled back, yanking his shorts off. He wore a knee-length bathing suit underneath his khaki cargo shorts. The suit was red with white flowers. He was chubby and slightly self-conscious about his flabby chest, so he kept his shirt on.

"Pokka pokka!" he shouted when he finally kicked his flip-flops off onto the curly Bermuda grass that covered the backyard of his grandmother's canal-side cottage.

"Pokka pokka!" Robby White answered back, treading water.

Pokka pokka had no meaning at all. It was just something they said to each other. They had been friends since fourth grade and *pokka pokka* was a little gag line that could mean just about anything.

You're an idiot.

I like it.

More, please.

No way.

It was a form of friend echolocation. Like bats sending

out pings—they could always track each other down by calling out to each other.

Jason ran toward the water. He was shorter than Robby, and not as athletic, but his weight gave him an advantage when it came to cannonballs. His feet made flat, flumping sounds as they hit the Tyvek boards of the pier. He almost tripped in his excitement, but luckily caught himself exactly as he neared the last board. Stumbling, he righted himself just enough to jump. It wasn't a great jump, but it was high enough to allow him to bring his knees against his chest. A second later the water exploded when his rear end hit the surface. His landing made a deep thudding sound, and he bobbed up almost immediately, his right hand coming up to wipe the water from his eyes.

"That's what I'm talking about!" he shouted.

Then he remembered it was dinnertime, twilight, and his grandmother had told him he could go swimming, but he shouldn't make a racket. You had to be considerate of your neighbors on the canal.

"Florida! Freaking Florida!" Robby said back to him. "I mean, how long were we in that car?"

"It was forever, man. I never thought we were getting here."

Robby swam a little closer to Jason. He whispered.

"Your mother is the slowest driver on earth, dude."

"I know, I know. She's ridiculous," Jason said.

"And when you get to Florida, you think, okay, we made it, but then Florida goes on a million miles!"

"Pokka pokka," Jason agreed.

They treaded water side by side for a moment.

"How nice is this water?" Robby asked.

"I *told* you! I told you it was nice down here. We can swim whenever we want."

"Living the life!" Robby said, treading water and lifting his body slightly above the surface. "I can't get over how warm it is . . ."

"It's pretty sweet. You got to listen to me sometimes! I tell you stuff and you don't listen."

"I'm listening," Robby said, then changed the subject. "Hey, you ever get any pythons around here? I heard Florida has gone crazy with pythons."

"And monitor lizards," Jason said, feeling his arms starting to tire. "People get bored with them as pets and let them

4

go wild, but it's mostly down in the Everglades."

"But they could be here, right, man?"

Jason shrugged. The talk in Florida about creatures potentially existing in the water always made him nervous. Always. Big creatures, big rib-cracking snakes. He had been coming to his grandma's over February break for a bunch of years, but he had never been entirely comfortable in the water. He had pretended to be comfortable, telling his mom he couldn't wait to get there, but Robby had touched a nerve. You didn't know what kinds of toothy animals lived in the canals or in the swamps or even at the beaches. It was hot in Florida, which meant animals could thrive. Robby wasn't wrong and he wasn't being paranoid. Florida had some serious creatures that could easily eat you.

"Get out if you're chicken," Jason said, knowing that it was easier to tease than to admit his own fears.

"I'm not chicken. I'm just saying."

"If you're not chicken, swim across the canal and come back."

"I'm not swimming across the canal, pokka."

"I knew you were chicken, man. I knew you would be."

Jason tucked his lips over his teeth and pretended to be

an animal ready to devour his friend. He reached over to grab Robby, but Robby ducked away.

"How deep is this thing, anyway?" Robby asked, looking back and forth from the dock to the other side of the canal. More houses lined the other side. Almost every house had a dock sticking out into the water, usually with a large motorboat attached to it.

"I don't know, honestly. I think they keep it dredged for the boats."

"And it connects right to the ocean?"

"Right to the ocean. I mean, through a bay and all. I don't know exactly."

Jason swam to the small metal ladder bolted to the side of his grandma's dock. He had been up and down that ladder a million times, he guessed.

"You're not getting out already, are you?" Robby asked.

"Swim across the canal if you're so gung ho, pokka. Let's see it."

"Tomorrow. Tomorrow I'll do it."

Jason made chicken squawks. He swung his butt onto the end of the pier and flapped his arms like wings. Robby grabbed his foot and tried to drag him back in the water, but

Jason snagged the top bend of the ladder and fended him off with his other leg.

"Let's go get some snacks," Jason said. "My grandma has, like, a thousand things in the house to eat."

"She loves her baby boy."

Jason shrugged.

"Maybe I'll swim across just because," Robby said, letting go of the dock beside Jason's foot. "Here I go. I'm like a dolphin."

He made a dolphin sound, a high, squeaky call. It was pretty accurate.

Robby swam on his back straight away from the pier. Jason watched him and realized it felt good to be in Florida. It felt normal. Having Robby along was a plus. Robby could drive, for one thing, and he had a way of making things fun.

Even now, just being an idiot, he stopped in the water and looked around.

"Something just rammed me!" he said, his mouth rounding in a circle of surprise. "Something under the water."

"*Riiiiiight,*" Jason said, running the word out with sarcasm.

"I mean it. Something just . . . geez!"

He began splashing water every which way, and Jason shook his head. *That's* what made Robby fun. He could turn even a stupid evening swim into a story. He was always doing something like that.

But then Jason saw something red blossom around Robby's body.

Instinctively, Jason pulled his feet away from the water.

"What . . . ," he started to ask, but then he saw Robby's eyes.

Robby's eyes weren't joking. Robby's eyes had gone wild and terrified.

Jason saw a large dark body, a fish's body, slash across Robby's chest and bite him on the shoulder. Then the shark dropped into the water and moved away. Its fin cleaved the water as it made its way across the canal. Then it seemed to reconsider. It turned quickly and stitched its way back toward Robby. The shark went underwater when it came to Robby. Robby jerked hard when the shark struck him again.

Jason stood quickly, his hand locked to the railing of the ladder.

Then Robby screamed.

"Shark! Shark!"

He screamed a hundred times, it seemed like. He tried to do a doggy paddle, but his body jerked from below.

Jason became aware that other people, people in houses up and down the canal, suddenly had them on their radar. That scream wasn't a fun scream. He heard people shout in response. He heard a screen door slam and someone wearing keys, or carrying keys, jingled toward them. But he couldn't turn his eyes away to see.

The shark rocketed up through the water and landed on Robby's shoulder and seemed to push him under purposely. As if escorting him under the waves.

It was a big shark, thick and dark. Its eye stared calmly at Jason as if suggesting he might be next. Robby tried to push the shark away, fending it off with his arms. The shark seemed to grow more determined. It fell back in the water, but kept surging forward, grabbing for anything with its deep, wide mouth.

For an instant, Jason thought about diving in to help his friend. He kept his eyes closed, hoping, somehow, that this had been a dream.

Barn Whimbril watched his mother set her right foot against her left calf and hold her hands in a prayer fashion against her chest. She stood on her yoga mat on the back porch of their cottage in Sarasota, Florida, greeting the sun. That's what she called it, anyway. Sun salutations.

Sometimes Barn did yoga with his mom, but not today.

Today was the opening of spring training in Fort Myers for the Boston Red Sox. And to Barn Whimbril, it was the best day of the year.

"Barn?" his mother called. "Check the oatmeal, would you? I think it's ready."

"Are you almost finished?"

"We have plenty of time. The game isn't until one."

Barn's rule number one with his mother: *You couldn't rush her.* He was aware that she had a different attitude about time than he did. A very different attitude. She was a hippie type, honestly, who had recently let her hair go gray, and now she wore it in a dense, tight braid in back. She liked to say she took the long view. Almost everything humans deemed important, or worth hurrying about, his mother saw as laughable.

"It's ready," Barn called, lifting the top off the pot of oatmeal and stirring it to check its viscosity. That meant how thick it was. Barn learned that last year in his fifth-grade science class.

"Serve it up, then. Come on out and we'll eat on the porch."

Barn nodded and opened the cupboard next to the sink to get bowls. For a second he caught his reflection in the small mirror his mother had attached to the back of the cupboard door. She used it to check her look some mornings when they had to hustle or when someone unexpectedly knocked at the door. Now, bending so he could see himself squarely in the mirror, he realized, for the millionth time, that he still resembled an angry rooster. Not just any rooster, either. He looked like a Rhode Island Red, the kind of chickens they had once raised in Pennsylvania before they moved down to Florida. His face was narrow and long, like a bird's face before it pecked, and his hair stuck up on top of his head like a rooster craw. He had white skin, pale, and rusty-colored hair. Hair the color of a steel wool pad after it had been used to clean four or five skillets. Skin the color of milk.

He thought about how Margaret Valley, the smartest and most beautiful girl in Sarasota's sixth-grade class, had once told her friend Becky Haller that she found his looks *interesting. What in the world*, he wondered as he pulled out two white bowls and put them on the tray they used to carry things outside, *did it mean to look interesting?*

He placed the oatmeal on the tray, placed a small pitcher of cream beside it along with a bowl of brown sugar, and then pushed backward through the screen door and stepped out onto the deck.

"What a day," his mom said.

She stood in the sun, her hands still in front of her chest, her right foot still locked against her left calf. She smiled.

She always smiled, Barn knew. She always seemed to be in a good mood. Today she was in an especially good mood because it was winter break for both of them. No school for a week.

"I have everything," Barn said, putting the food on the circular glass table they kept on the porch. "If we're going to make the game, we need to keep moving."

"We're not leaving for another hour, Barn."

True, Barn conceded. He knew he was a little keyed up. He sat in one of the porch chairs and scooped out two bowls of oatmeal. He remembered, too late, that his mother had told him to bring out raisins to add. He popped up and went inside and came back with the raisins from Holly's Universal Galactic Health Food. Everything they ate, just about, came from Holly's Universal Galactic Health Food Store. Holly was a friend of his mom's. The monogram for the store, used on bags and cartons, was HUG. Holly's Universal Galactic.

"I'm almost done. I'm just doing a little ujjayi breathing."

Nostril breathing, Barn knew. She performed ujjayi breathing at the end of her practice with her eyes closed.

"The oatmeal will get cold."

"I like it a little cold. It's like eating paste."

"You're weird, Mom."

Barn ate a few spoons of his oatmeal before his mom finally rolled up her mat and came to sit beside him. Before she did, she put her arms around Barn and kissed his cheek. Barn flinched a little, but he knew that would encourage his mother to kiss him more. She always kissed and hugged him and told him she loved him. If he recoiled at all, or became impatient, she lathered it on even more. She was a tidal wave of mom-ness.

"You excited?" she asked when she settled beside him. "Opening day."

"Yep."

He kept his eyes on his bowl of oatmeal. She was just warming up.

"You still a Red Sox fan?" she asked. "You haven't changed loyalties, have you?"

He nodded. Then shook his head. He wasn't sure which question he needed to answer first. His mom kept going, anyway.

"How do you root for the Boston Red Sox when you live down here in Florida?"

"Because they have spring training here, Mom. And because Dad loved the Sox."

"I know," she said, and reached over to squeeze his hand. "Just checking on you."

She didn't follow baseball at all except for the spring training games that took place near Sarasota. She went to those games for him, Barn understood, because she knew he loved them. This was the fifth year they'd been going—ever since his dad had been killed in Afghanistan. Mostly she read novels at the spring games. She was an English teacher at Sarasota High School. She read as routinely as other people breathed.

"You're in charge of loading the car, Barn," she said as she finished eating. "Sunblock, chairs, maybe a picnic blanket. You know, the usual stuff. Try not to forget anything. Go, Sox."

"Go, Sox."

"Eat your breakfast," his mom said, pushing back his hair and kissing his forehead as she rose.

He did. He watched a phoebe—a small gray songbird easily recognizable for its habit of bobbing its tail up and down—building a nest on the doorjamb above their toolshed. Phoebes were a sure sign of spring. A week before, he had set up a tiny camera on the nesting platform and put the feed on YouTube. So far he'd had 7,432 visitors. He figured once the eggs started hatching, he would get more views. He had sent a link to the Florida Audubon Society. His whole class knew about the site, and his teacher, Ms. Ellsbury, had given him extra credit in honors science for setting it up.

Barn finished eating and stacked the dishes on the tray. He backed through the door and rinsed everything in the sink. He put his Red Sox hat on and bent to look at himself again in the mirror.

The sight was remarkable.

A Rhode Island rooster wearing a hat, he thought. A bird rooting for a baseball team.

In that moment his phone played the *Jaws* theme.

Duh duh. Dun duh dun duh dun duh, faster and faster.

Only one message triggered that music. Shark attack.

He ran to get his phone.

Barn kept his bedroom dim. He had six separate aquariums bubbling from different surfaces in his room. The aquariums gave him enough light and they also made him feel like he was underwater. It was goofy and probably a little weird, but that's how it felt.

When he scrambled into his room—the walls covered with a Boston Red Sox pennant, a picture of his mom, a painting by his aunt Jupiter, and a huge poster of a white shark breaching with a seal in its mouth—he felt himself calm. Water did that to him.

Around the room his six aquariums were stocked with fish. One freshwater, five salt. Two of the aquariums held nothing but black-banded cat sharks, a fairly common aquarium shark easily recognizable for its large zebra stripes. Cat sharks, from the family Scyliorhinidae, could also be known as dogfish, which confused just about every one. Those he traded or sold. He had two aquariums with a combination of rare wobbegongs—bearded, paisley-skinned Australian sharks—and brown-banded bamboo sharks. Barn was fascinated by their alternating stripes of white and brown. He also had a dozen epaulette sharks, sharks with a pair of distinctive black disks on their shoulders, scouring the bottoms of his tanks. They were all hungry most of the time, all sharks in miniature.

That boy should have a pair of gills, his aunt Jupiter said whenever she spent any time around him.

He kind of agreed with her. Gills would be amazing.

He sat down at his desk and opened the message from the Global Shark Attack File. Barn subscribed to the Global Shark Attack site and received notices when a human/shark interaction took place anywhere around the world. He loved getting updates from GSAF.

It was an incident report about a shark attack in a Florida canal. Barn had read a thousand of these over the last five years, ever since he first discovered the site when he was seven.

Activity: Evening swim.

Case: GSAF 2019 02-788

Date: Feb. 22, 2020

Location: The incident took place in Apple Way Canal, four miles north of Port Charlotte, Florida. Charlotte County, Florida, USA

Name of Victim: Robby White

Description: 17-year-old male from Plainfield, New Jersey

Background Weather: The air temperature at Apple Way Canal was 76 degrees F. Local stations report cloudy skies with a dew point of 60 F, humidity 84%, seal level pressure 28.6, and a slight breeze (1 mph) from the north.

Moon Phase: Three-quarter waxing moon.

Sea Conditions: Mean low tide occurred at 05h24, mean high tide at 12h04.

Distance from Shore: 20 feet, a third of the way across the canal.

Depth of Water: 14 feet

Time: 7:45 p.m.

Narrative: It was the first day in Florida for two New Jersey boys. They were visiting one of the boys' grandmothers. They went in for a swim after a long drive from New Jersey. The victim yelled about being bumped by something. Moments later, according to witness Jason St. John, the shark attacked. The length of the incident was approximately five minutes.

Injuries: Massive. Concentration of wounds on upper torso. Fatal. Died on way to the hospital.

First Aid: Medical attention received.

Species: According to witness, the shark was about 9 feet in length.

Case Investigator: Melissa Jordan, GSAF

Barn read the incident report three times. A fatal attack always made Barn feel deep sorrow. At the same time, he understood sharks weren't evil. They had reasons to attack. Something had to trigger the attack. During his last time through the report, he felt himself drifting. He imagined himself in the water with a shark, an attacking shark. He wondered if he would panic. He wondered what Robby White had thought about when he realized that a shark had bitten him.

He forwarded the incident report to Lucas Iglesias, shark lover and owner of AQUATARIUM, the best fish store in the Sarasota area. Before he could put down his phone, Lucas replied.

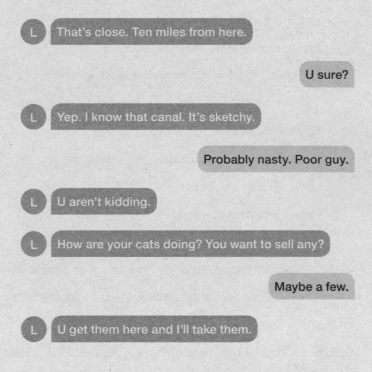

L That's close. Ten miles from here.

U sure?

L Yep. I know that canal. It's sketchy.

Probably nasty. Poor guy.

L U aren't kidding.

L How are your cats doing? You want to sell any?

Maybe a few.

L U get them here and I'll take them.

Barn heard his mother coming down the hallway. Their

house was old for Florida and built of repurposed construction wood, and it made a sound like a boat when anyone walked around in it. He put his phone down.

"Who's slowing things down now?" she asked, sticking her head in the door.

"Sorry. Feeding the fish."

"Baseball today. Fish tomorrow."

"What if we didn't go to the game today?"

She looked puzzled. She came in and sat on the edge of his bed. He didn't know what he wanted to say exactly, but it felt strange to be going to a baseball game when a shark attack had taken place less than ten miles away.

"What's going on?" she asked softly.

"There was a shark attack close by. Not far from here."

"Okay . . ."

"I thought maybe . . ."

"What did you think, sweetheart?"

"I thought that I might be able to help."

"How would you help?"

"I'm not sure. Somebody died and I know a lot about sharks."

"You can say that again. Sometimes I think you are a shark."

"I just thought if I could see where it took place . . . I might be able to help somehow. Maybe stop it from happening again?"

"Are you sure? You love the Sox."

"I know, but this . . ."

"Is a shark attack," she completed his thought for him. "Yep, I get it. Okay, one deal. You do not go into the water. Understood?"

"Yes."

"What don't you do?"

"Go into the water."

"And you are sensitive to the situation. When did this happen?"

"Last night. In the evening."

"Well, people are probably going to be upset. You need to use good social skills, okay? Read the situation. Don't ask too many questions, if you know what I mean."

"I'll be careful."

"And what don't you do?"

"Go into the water."

"Want to go to the Sox later in the week?"

"Maybe. I kind of want to see this through."

She stood and came next to him. She bent close to the tank of bamboo sharks and watched.

"What do you love about them so much, Barn?"

"Their form. They've had the same form for a million years. And the way they swim."

"You love their grace."

"I guess."

"Stay out of the water," she said, and kissed his cheek. "That's the deal."

She walked out. He leaned across his desk and put his forehead close to the tank of bamboo sharks, just as his mom had done. He watched the sharks. They had the perfect form, the perfect grace. He pictured them bigger, a thousand times bigger, their tails thrashing hard as they surged through the water after him.

3

Barn climbed on his Swagtron EB6 Electric Fat Bike and looked behind him to make sure the bags of banded cat sharks hadn't shifted. He had equipped the back rack of the bike with a milk crate and had rigged up a cardboard cover to keep the sun off the fish. He had transported sharks in aquarium bags before on the Swagtron, but it always made him nervous. The fish were as comfortable as they could be, given that they had been yanked out of their environment and placed in plastic bags. Fish hated travel. He didn't blame them.

Barn sat on the seat and pedaled. He wore a light fisherman's shirt, long sleeves, and white cotton pants. He tucked a large red bandana under the back of his Red Sox hat so that it covered his neck. He had applied zinc oxide to his nose and had lathered himself with sunblock. He looked ridiculous, he was sure, but what could he do?

He switched on the electric motor when he had gone a half block toward the AQUATARIUM. The fat bike began to purr and the bandana on his neck flew up and flapped in the early morning breeze.

Five miles and several minutes later, he pulled into the parking lot of the AQUATARIUM and found Lucas Iglesias's legs sticking out from underneath a twenty-four-foot Chris-Craft boat. Lucas bought and sold used boats in addition to running the best pet fish store in the area. He was constantly working on equipment. Barn turned off the Swagtron's engine while Lucas wiggled his body out from under the boat. He sat up and mopped his face with a large red towel.

"Look at you!" Lucas said, smiling. "Why your mom decided to bring her redheaded son to live in the Florida heat I'll never understand."

Barn grinned.

"You should ask her. I wonder the same thing all the time. Did you buy that boat?"

"Not yet. I'm looking her over. Did you bring the cats?"

"In the basket."

"Let's get them inside out of the sun."

Barn put the Swagtron on its kickstand and folded back the cardboard cover from the milk crate. Lucas stood and came to look at them. Barn was surprised to find he was now officially taller than Lucas, despite Lucas being twice as old. Lucas carried weight down low, around his hips, and his arms were muscular and heavy from working with his hands. He always wore shorts, usually blue work shorts, and a pair of flip-flops. He had come to Florida from Panama. His parents still lived in Panama, although Lucas talked about bringing them to Florida.

"They look good," Lucas said, bending over to inspect the banded cats. "Let's get them in a tank."

Barn followed Lucas into the AQUATARIUM. It was delicious to step out of the harsh morning sun and enter the cool, dark environment of the store. It was one of Barn's favorite places. He had to stop and let his eyes adjust before he could follow Lucas into the work area behind the cash register. Lucas lifted up the bag he carried and carefully floated it in a large fifty-gallon tank. Barn put his bag into the tank beside the first one. He stood beside Lucas for a while and watched the sharks patrolling the interior wall of the plastic bags.

"It never gets old," Lucas said. "Does it?"

"Never," Barn agreed.

"Just the way they swim."

"I know."

Lucas went to his cash register and popped it open.

"I'm paying sixty a cat. You have four. Do you want credit or cash?"

"Cash, please."

Lucas lifted the interior of the cash box and counted out $240. He handed it to Barn. Barn folded the bills and put them in his front pocket. He had plans for the money, specifically a second bike battery, but he had to get his mom to drive him to downtown Sarasota for that errand.

"Nice fish," Lucas said. "I'll take as many as you can raise."

"Thanks, Lucas."

"You going up to look at that canal? Where the boy was attacked?"

"I planned to, yes."

"Don't do anything risky. I mean, stay out of the water until they do more investigation. It could be a deadly situation."

"I know. I'll be careful."

"You on your own? Where's Finn?"

Finn Moody was Barn's best friend. They always hung around together.

"He had to visit his grandparents in Tennessee. He'll be back tomorrow."

"I'd feel better if you had your sidekick with you."

"I'm just going to go look. It's vacation week. I have some time."

"I get that, but be careful. The shark that took that boy is no banded cat or bamboo shark."

Barn nodded. He knew that much. He had read every detail, every line of every story about the attack.

"I've got to get under that boat again before the sun gets too high. Take a look around. I've got some new tangs you might want to look at. Beautiful fish."

"Thanks, I will."

"It's my favorite time of day in here. It's quiet and calm. Later on the fish get more active."

After Lucas left the store, Barn walked slowly along the fish tanks. As usual, he admired the care that Lucas lavished on them. They were immaculate, for one thing. He did not overstock his tanks, nor did he put any artificial gizmos inside. No phony treasure chests or deep-sea divers trailing bubbles to the surface. No, his tanks spoke to a careful appreciation of fish and their habitats.

Barn found the new batch of tangs in the last tank on the left. He bent close to see them—blue tangs and sailfin tangs—and was still watching them when he saw the door to the shop open. He watched the door in the tank's reflection, a blast of sunlight, then two figures stepped inside. He couldn't help seeing his own reflection, his weird bandana sticking out from behind his hat, and he yanked the cloth off as he stood to see the customers.

Margaret Valley and her mother walked a few steps into the shop, their eyes obviously getting adjusted to the cool interior light. Barn felt his stomach roll and it became hard to swallow.

Margaret's mother called to him.

"Do you work here?"

He shook his head. He kept looking at the tangs, although

he could follow the two human-shaped reflections in the aquarium glass.

The Margaret reflection took a step closer.

"Barn?" she asked.

He couldn't hide any longer. He turned slowly. *A rooster looking at fish tanks*, he thought. That's what he looked like.

"Oh, hi, Margaret."

"Is this a friend of yours, Margaret?"

The mom walked toward him. Her heels clacked on the linoleum floor. She looked dressed up. She must also have been wearing a bucket of perfume, because he smelled it as she approached. Barn realized Margaret looked a lot like her mom. They both had straight black hair and big blue eyes. They both had excellent posture. Margaret's mom looked happy but busy, as if most of the time she had a to-do list and she wanted to check off items.

"Barn?" she asked, glancing back at her daughter. "Did I catch that right?"

"Yes, ma'am."

"Like a building on a farm?"

Barn nodded. He had explained the origin of his name

too many times to find the question interesting.

"How did you get a name like that? I bet it has a story behind it. Does it? I bet it does."

Barn wondered if he could go out the back way. If he could just run and hop onto the Swagtron and get out of there. But he was too polite for that.

"It was a nickname, really," Barn said. "My dad loved barns, so he named me after his favorite thing."

"Oh, well, isn't that wonderful? Margaret, did you know that about Barn?"

It was an awkward moment. Margaret had gone off down the far aisle to look at fish. Her mom tried to unite them by making comments and being friendly. Barn wanted to shrink down to fish size and dive into one of the aquariums.

"No, I didn't know," Margaret answered absently.

"Well, I think it's a wonderful name. A memorable name," Margaret's mom said, chipper as usual. "Now, maybe you could help us with a recommendation. We're looking for a fish for a cousin's birthday party. He's just getting started with his aquarium ... Do you know a lot about fish?"

Fortunately, Lucas showed up at that moment. Margaret's mom stopped and turned. Lucas smiled and came forward, wiping his hands again on the red towel. He was a good salesman, Barn knew.

"He's the owner," Barn said. "He'll know the best thing."

"Oh, hello," Margaret's mom said, slightly overfriendly. "We were just asking Barn about fish!"

Barn slid down the aisle. The only trouble was, he had to pass Margaret to make it out of the store. He wished he didn't look like a carrot.

"He'll help," Barn said, meaning Lucas would help them.

Meaning he had to leave.

Meaning he was flustered.

Meaning he felt too shy to say full sentences to Margaret.

But she surprised him.

"You having a good break?" she asked, turning from the nearest aquarium to meet his eyes.

"I guess. Are you?"

"We have to go to that birthday party. The kid is a monster."

"Oh," Barn said, edging past Margaret.

He couldn't think of a thing to say about that.

"You like fish?" she asked.

He nodded.

"My dad is big into snorkeling if you ever want to go out. He knows all the local reefs."

"Cool," Barn said.

"I never feel that comfortable in the water," she said. "I'm always looking over my shoulder, if you know what I mean."

"I do. It can be unsettling."

"Is that your bike outside?"

He nodded.

"It's electric, right? I wanted to get one of those. How many miles do you get?"

"About ten. A ten-mile range. If I can get another battery, then I'll double the range."

Margaret's mom called across the shop.

"Margaret, see what you think of this one," she said. "They're really beautiful."

"Have to go," Margaret said. "Duty calls."

Barn nodded. He wanted to think of something clever to say, something to make her remember him, but his brain felt like pudding.

He nearly stumbled getting out of the shop. For a moment

he stood in the bright sunlight, dazed to be out of the cool darkness. He climbed on the Swagtron as quickly as he could and kicked it into action. The engine began to purr. He felt all mixed up. He went almost a mile in the wrong direction before he shook himself and turned south, heading for Apple Way Canal and the scene of the attack.

4

Barn had to stop twice and check his phone to make sure he had the right coordinates for Apple Way Canal. Whole sections of Florida had been turned into the same landscape: canals snaking from the nearest water body in lazy Us or Cs, with houses built on top of them. That was what people wanted in Florida, he knew. They wanted water and they wanted to have their boats beside them. They wanted a sliding glass door and a small lawn and a place to put a picnic table. It almost didn't matter what the water was like, or how small the yard. As long as people had a sliver of water, they seemed to be happy.

That meant there were a lot of canals to investigate. It

also meant that sharks and tarpon and giant goliaths had perfect breeding grounds right outside people's doors.

It was close to noon when he finally found Apple Way Canal. He almost passed it by, but then did a quick U-turn and read the green street sign that marked the entrance to the road that paralleled the water. Apple Way. He turned his engine off and used the bike's pedals instead. He wanted to take it slow. He also wanted to conserve his battery.

It wasn't easy to get close to the water. The houses blocked access and they were built side by side, tiny yards connecting them. Most of the yards had chain-link fences dividing them from their neighbors. Many houses had solar panels wedged into the yards wherever they could point the panels south.

He had biked nearly a quarter mile down Apple Way when he found a boat ramp that obviously provided access to the water. He stopped beside it. Someone had posted a sign that said WATER CLOSED, then had a triangular figure of a person swimming with a big red slash through it. The meaning was obvious.

No swimming.

It didn't say why. Maybe because, Barn figured, the

homeowners didn't want their addresses known as a place where sharks ate people.

He climbed off his bike and walked it toward the boat ramp. He leaned the bike on the CLOSED FOR SWIMMING sign and stood for a moment gazing as far as he could in both directions. It looked like a thousand other canals around Florida. It was forty feet across, maybe more, with wooden retaining walls establishing the land where the houses existed.

He was still standing near the water when an old Ford pickup began backing up to use the boat ramp. The driver had a square johnboat—a flat-bottomed rowboat—in the pickup bed. A fisherman. Barn moved to one side and let the driver have access to the water. The driver backed until his rear tires were six inches into the canal. The force of the tires sent a ripple across the flat, shiny water.

"Give me a hand?" the driver asked, climbing out. "I can do it myself, but it's sure a lot easier with a second pair of hands."

He was an older black man with gray hair and a slight limp in his right leg. He wore a Braves hat and old-people sunglasses, the kind that fit over regular glasses. His T-shirt had a big fish hook on the front, but no lettering. Khaki shorts and water sandals.

"Sure," Barn answered. "What do you want me to do?"

"Just wait a second until I undo the ropes. Then we just lift it out."

Barn nodded. He watched the man work at the ropes. Barn stepped closer to the truck and worked on his side.

"Harry," the man said, his hands busy, "that's my name."

"Barn."

"Bernard?"

"No, Barn, like a building."

"You come from farming people?"

"No, my mom . . . it's a long story."

Harry nodded. He pulled off a thick rope and rounded it out in his hands. He put it in the truck bed and then stepped to the back of the truck. He put a plank against the tailgate so the boat could slide down it.

"If you can handle that side, I can take this one," Harry said.

"Got it."

The boat slid out easily. Once the stern floated, the rest came forward in one good glide. The boat drifted out into the canal. Harry retrieved it by the painter line—a rope connected to the bow—and docked the boat on the ramp.

"Thank you, young man," Harry said, extending one hand to Barn.

Barn shook it. The man had heavy hands, rough hands toughened by work.

"You're not planning on swimming, are you?" Harry asked, lifting his fishing gear out of the truck and stowing it in the boat. "I wouldn't advise it. News crews were up here just the other day setting right up where you're standing."

"The shark attack?"

"That's right. You count about three houses up, that's the spot. Sad thing is, I could have told them. Anyone who fishes around here could have told them."

"About the sharks?"

Harry laughed softly and shook his head.

"Better believe it. I get a good snook or tarpon on, it's a race to get it into the boat before a shark takes it. I've seen the sharks, believe me. They swim right under the boat and look at me like I'm dinner."

"Do you know what kind?"

"Not sure. People say different things. Heck, there was a guy here on the canal, he's quoted in the paper as saying the attack was probably a white shark. I don't know much, but I know no white sharks are swimming up here and waiting for kids to swim."

"Was it always a dangerous canal?"

"No, just in the past year or so. Something changed," Harry said, lifting a gas can into the back of the boat. "The water seems busier. More going on down below. The fishing is good, though. No complaint about that."

"Do you just fish the canal here?"

"Here, and sometimes I go out into the bay."

"It connects?"

"If you know what you're doing, it does. It's a little tricky and on a low tide it gets dicey. Boats hang up all the time. I don't have much draft on this one, so I can go through in any kind of situation."

"So sharks could swim up here?"

"Easy as pie," Harry said, stretching his back after he had settled the gas can in the boat. "They can come in even on a low tide. Probably follow the fish in and out. These people don't know it, but building where they do, they're inviting the wolf to their front doors. I feel terrible about that boy, but it was bound to happen sooner or later. I don't go in the water myself. I know too much."

Barn nodded. It *was* a jungle under the surface. People didn't realize it, but Harry was correct. Eat or be eaten, that was the rule under the water. Before Barn could say anything else, a half dozen small tarpon suddenly scattered on the surface out beyond the ramp. They jumped and ran, dotting the water in an explosive run. Harry pointed to them.

"Just what we're talking about. Something chased them and they took off. People see that and get excited about the fish, but they forget to think about what was down under the surface chasing them. Bigger fish eat littler fish. It's the way of the world."

Harry said he had to pull his truck into the parking area. Barn waited by the boat. When Harry came back, he had put on a fishing vest over his T-shirt. The vest had a bunch of flies and lures attached to the top pocket. The lures caught the light and shimmered.

"Do you have much luck midday?" Barn asked. "Isn't it better to fish at sunset?"

"It is better, but this is the time I have. Out in the bay I usually do okay around this time. It's just a chance to get away, that's all."

"Want me to push you off?"

"Sure, thanks. Nice talking to you, Barn. That's a strange name, that one. But, sure, yes, please push me off once I get settled by the engine. Don't get any ideas about going into this water, you hear me? I know young people can't resist a challenge sometimes."

"I won't, I promise."

"There's a guy up there who wants to dynamite the whole thing. That's an ignorant attitude. Things aren't usually made better by dynamite."

"Not usually."

Barn waited for the sign. When Harry checked everything one last time, he pulled the engine starter. It bubbled right up. He nodded to Barn and Barn pushed the boat straight back. Harry waited for the momentum to stop before he turned the engine throttle and started down the canal toward the bay.

Harry waved and Barn waved back. The wake behind the boat spread and widened in bars of light and movement. Barn watched the boat putter down the canal until it disappeared around a corner. Afterward, he went back to the Swagtron and grabbed a bottle of water from the storage compartment. Something about the change in angle made him see a second sign, this one nailed into a tree at the water's edge. It looked like a quick job, a temporary sign hung up for special circumstances.

CAUTION (¡PRECAUCIÓN!)
Swim at Your Own Risk
(NADE BAJO SU PROPIO RIESGO)
Keep Away from Marine Wildlife
(MANTENERSE ALEJADO DE LA VIDA MARINA)
CONFIRMED SHARK ATTACK (ATAQUE DE TIBURÓN CONFIRMADO)

5

Barn stood in the midday sun, aware that he was beginning to fry. He wasn't sure what he wanted to do now that he had found the canal. He wished he could lift the surface of the water and peer beneath it.

Barn looked up and down the canal as far as he could see. After staring for a few minutes, he discovered a path on the other side. It wasn't much of a walkway, that was for sure. It looked left over from an earlier building plan. It was partially wood, partially cement, and it was only a few feet wide at its broadest point. But it ran along the canal for as far as he could see. It was the best access he was likely to find.

He climbed on the Swagtron and kicked it into motion. The engine began to purr. He rode south along the edge of the canal, searching for a way to cross it. He didn't find one. Not at first, anyway. He came to a 7-Eleven parking lot and cut across it. He had to travel two blocks in the wrong direction before he found the road running down the opposite side of Apple Way Canal. After that, he turned off the motor and pedaled. It was hot as an oven on the bike, in the road, midday. No shade. He promised himself he would put on sunblock the next time he stopped.

Eventually he spotted the boat ramp from his vantage point across the canal. He put his feet down to the ground on either side of the bike and counted up from the ramp. Three houses, Harry had said. In the end, he realized, he couldn't have missed it, because yellow police tape still fluttered on the dock at the point where Robby White had been attacked.

"Dang," he whispered.

Seeing the yellow tape made it real.

He took out his phone and snapped a half-dozen photos. He texted them to Finn Moody and Lucas Iglesias. Lucas's return text came almost at once.

Gnarly.

Fisherman said this place is sharky.

 I believe it. Keep your feet dry.

I will.

 You thinking bull shark, right?

Barn sent back an emoji of a shrug. Then he put his phone away.

He leaned his bike against a telephone pole and began working his way slowly up the walkway bordering the canal. The walkway wasn't terribly narrow, but the fact that the water below him contained sharks made him slightly nervous. He didn't want to fall in; that was a given. The shark that had killed Robby White was probably not gone. Or alone. Everything considered, the conditions in the canal were perfect for a bull shark. For many bull sharks.

He paid attention to the water. He paid so much attention that he didn't see the German shepherd that suddenly sprinted across the lawn of the house and came flying up at him. The dog put his paws on the chain-link fence that kept him inside, his mouth open, his bark rapid and fierce.

Barn almost stumbled into the water. The dog growled at him. It was a black kind of German shepherd, slick and lethal-looking. Barn steadied himself, glancing at the water for a second.

"You coming to gawk?" a voice asked. "That dog is a public nuisance, but he can't get out."

It was a man's voice.

Barn looked around. The direct sun and the growling dog made him a little dizzy. He put his hand up like a visor and looked around. The voice reached him again.

"Down here," the man said.

The voice belonged to an older white guy. He stood in a vintage Stingray, a twenty-six-footer, Barn guessed, and he was working on something in the steering column. He had a tool chest open beside him. Part of the steering column had been removed and a bunch of wires sprouted out like the leafy part of a celery stalk. The man looked like a lot of men looked down in Florida. He was somewhere around seventy, Barn supposed, and thin in his legs and butt, but he carried a plump belly that folded over his belt. He wore shorts and a cotton shirt and a baseball hat that said WORLD'S BEST GRANDPA on the front.

He pointed a pair of spanners—large pliers—at Barn the next time he spoke.

"Heck of a thing," the man said. "Happened right here. Not just an old canal anymore, is it? Gives the water a whole new meaning, doesn't it?"

"I guess so."

"You guess so?" the man asked, his voice rising. "A boy died here. You don't seem to understand."

Barn quartered around so that the sun wasn't in his eyes. The old man waved the spanners at the water.

"Why aren't you in school, anyway?"

"We have a week off."

"You kids have so much time off these days . . . it's always a vacation."

"It's just a week off," Barn said, thinking how his mother would go off on this guy if she heard him.

"Oh, teachers' meetings and professional development days. Don't think I don't know what goes on in a school."

Barn squatted down and poked his chin at the steering column.

"You having problems with that?"

"This? You better believe it."

"My friend could fix that in no time."

"What friend is that?"

"His name is Finn Moody. He's kind of like an electronics genius."

"You don't say?" the man said, and he seemed to take a deep breath. "Where's this kid live?"

"He's up in Tennessee visiting his grandparents right now, but he'll be back tomorrow. He's local."

"You really think he could fix this?"

"He can fix almost anything."

The man pursed his lips.

Barn knew the best way to deal with old people was to help them out, or let them see you cared. Then they wanted to be your best buddy. Florida had a zillion old people walking around and you had to remember how to handle them. If you went at it wrong, they could be grumpy as anything. Barn always tried to be polite and helpful.

"Well, you bring this Finn by if you want to. This steering column is more than I can handle."

"He can fix it. He's worked on a lot of boats with his dad."

"Tell him I'll pay him."

Barn nodded. Finn made good money doing projects exactly like this one.

"My grandkids call me Grandpa Lemon, because my last name is Lemon. I'm here most days working on this."

"Barn Whimbril," Barn said. "Nice to meet you."

"Did you say Barn?"

Barn nodded. The man looked at him carefully.

"Well, that's a new one on me. To each his own, I always say. You thirsty? Here, have a water," the man said, and dug out a plastic water bottle from a cooler at his feet and tossed it to Barn. Barn caught it. He was thirsty, and the water felt good and cold in his hand, but he tossed the bottle back to the old man.

"Thanks anyway, but I'm not thirsty."

"Everyone's thirsty in Florida. What, are you some environmental nut?"

"I try not to use plastic bottles. Sorry."

The man deliberately screwed off the bottle top. He looked at Barn, then tilted the bottle to his lips. He drank almost half the bottle, then put it down and smacked his lips.

"You sure, cowboy?"

"I'm sure. Could you tell me, have there been shark

problems before this attack?" Barn asked when he thought enough time had gone by so that he wouldn't look too eager.

"In this canal? Not so you would notice. I mean, I suppose anything is possible. But you don't expect a shark to come this far inland."

Barn nodded. The man had no idea.

"They caught a bull shark in Illinois one time. It came all the way up the Mississippi River and raided some fish traps."

"How many miles?"

Barn shrugged. He wasn't sure and he didn't like to make up information he didn't have.

"A long way. I think around seven hundred miles. They go up rivers and up canals."

"I know," the man said. "But this had to be a sizable shark. I didn't expect big sharks to come in here."

"Have you seen any other activity?"

"Why are you asking?"

"I find sharks interesting."

Grandpa Lemon reached down and finished off his bottle of water.

"I don't go in the water," he said, "and I don't let any of my grandkids swim here. To be honest, I don't like the look of the water in this canal. Too dark and quiet. Kind of spooky. I take my grandkids to the beach. They like having the waves better, anyway."

"But people swim here, right?"

"Not anymore."

"But before the attack?"

Grandpa Lemon shrugged again. He looked across the canal at the house with yellow tape and then stepped across the boat to whisper.

"She doesn't go in the water. She doesn't know the water. She never should have had those kids swimming in there."

"You mean . . ."

"I mean the kid's grandma. The one they were visiting. She doesn't own a boat or anything. She kind of lost track of what was going on in the canal. I guess she wanted the boys to have a good time, so she just let them swim. She probably didn't think a thing about it."

Barn nodded. He stood and felt the sun make him a bit dizzier. It was time to find shade. He told Grandpa Lemon that he would be by again with Finn.

"You bring him and I'll make it worth his while if he's as good as you say."

"I will."

"An electronics genius, eh? That would be a miracle. This steering column is going to kill me."

"He'll fix it, believe me."

"Okay, bring him by."

Barn said goodbye, then walked back to his Swagtron and mounted it. He sat for a minute to get his balance. The picture of what had happened was becoming clear. He was still sitting on his bike making mental notes when he heard a splash and listened to a woman's voice calling loudly on the midday air.

"That's a girl, that's a girl, good girl."

Barn kicked the Swagtron into motion. As the bike picked up speed, he saw the boat ramp across the canal. It flashed at him between spaces made by the yards as the bike began to move. Standing on the ramp, a young woman with a dog leash rocked back and threw a tennis ball into the water. Barn watched a golden retriever dive into the water and begin swimming like an arrow to the center of the canal.

"Get the dog out of the water! Get her out!" Barn yelled.

But nobody heard him.

The shark did not think when it heard the dog enter the water.

It did not reason.

It thought of food and danger. It did not wish to harm anyone. It merely wished to eat, to satisfy the hunger that forced it to search endlessly for nourishment. Nourishment meant energy, and energy meant nourishment.

This was the animal that detected the golden retriever paddling across the canal to retrieve a tennis ball.

The paddle strokes of the dog's four paws moved the water, which in turn sent vibrations to the shark's lateral line, a system of sense organs used to detect movement and vibration and pressure gradients in the surrounding water. The shark locked on to the dog's location.

Two contrasting impulses entered the fish's calculations, both simple. The first was *food*. The shark lived by investigating movement. The second was *danger*. The shark survived by not putting itself in danger. To accommodate both impulses, the shark swam up from the bottom of the canal and passed once beneath the dog. It kept its distance. In the murky water, the shark had the benefit of ambush. It detected the creature above. It understood—at a primitive level—that the creature did not detect it swimming beneath it.

It passed six feet below the swimming dog. The depth of a grave.

On its second pass, it brushed against the dog's right front paw. The shark's skin—dermal denticles like hard, grooved teeth, which both protected the shark and made it more streamlined as it passed through the water—tingled. The shark's pace quickened. Its eyes peered through the murky water, trying to make sense of the dog's strange silhouette.

Food, the message confirmed.

The shark closed.

6

"Get away from there!"

Barn skidded to a stop and jumped off the Swagtron. The young woman with the leash took two steps sideways, obviously surprised and unnerved at his fast approach. She held up a hand as if he intended to jump on her. But Barn ran past her and began calling to the dog. He didn't know its name, but it didn't matter.

"Come here, girl, come here, come here," he chanted.

The dog swam toward him, a tennis ball in its mouth. It made a huffing sound, trying to breathe around the yellow ball. The dog was not far from shore. Barn waded in up to his ankles. He wanted to go deeper, but the promise he'd made to his mom stuck in his mind. No swimming, no water. He held out his hand to the dog.

"What are you doing?" the young woman asked, her voice rising. "Get away from my dog!"

"Come here, girl," Barn continued, concentrating. "That's a girl."

In that moment, he saw the shark.

It came like a deep, dark wish, a terror, a stalking dream. Barn watched the water bulge behind the dog. The shark was about six feet long. Maybe 290 or 300 pounds of sleek gray muscle. Its body was stout and abrupt. Barn grabbed a rock from the side of the boat ramp and threw it. He tossed it so it would go over the dog and land behind it, right where he knew the shark swam. The rock was fair-sized and it landed with a loud *kerplunk!*

Two things happened.

First, the clueless dog turned around as if Barn's rock toss had been another ball chucked into the water for it to fetch. It did that even with a tennis ball already wedged in its mouth.

It swam toward where the shark waited!

Second, the shark swam off. The rock scared it away.

Barn *saw it*, which was amazing. He noted that its tail fin was smaller than the prominent dorsal fin at the top of its body. It veered to the right and flicked its tail and disappeared instantly into deeper water.

"Come here," Barn said emphatically, and waded out knee deep.

The dog, ridiculously, could not find the ball. It couldn't find it because it was a rock, not a ball. *Duh.* But as a retriever the dog stayed paddling back and forth, its head turning to see where the ball had gone. The tips of its ears lay flat against the water.

"Get it onshore!" Barn said sharply to the woman.

"Get away from my dog!"

"There's a shark in there!" Barn said, trying to keep himself calm but serious, and he saw the young woman's eyes reveal doubt. "I'm not kidding! Didn't you see the signs? A shark made a run at your dog already! I'm not joking!"

The young woman moved around him, still wary. She dug in her pocket and came out with a biscuit.

"Come here, Bonnie," the young woman said.

The dog turned slowly toward shore. Barn watched. He didn't know if the shark would come back to make a second run at the dog. If it did, the dog was a goner. First time bump, second time chomp. That's what sharks did.

The dog finally found its feet on the ramp. Barn squatted next to the dog, trying to remove the sun's reflection from his line of vision. He saw the shark again, this time farther out from shore, deeper, its body a dark line of lethal muscle. He grabbed the dog's collar and walked firmly to its owner.

The young woman got the dog to take the biscuit. In almost the same motion, she clipped the dog's leash onto its collar. The dog dropped the ball in the choppy wash of its splashing, waiting for someone to throw the ball again.

"You can't let her swim here," Barn said. "Something's going . . ."

The woman didn't answer. She looked angry. He realized now that she wore a uniform of some sort. An orange apron hung around her neck with the name of a home repair shop across her chest. Maybe she was on break from work, he decided. Maybe she just wanted to give the dog a break from the day's heat. In any case, she walked the dog rapidly back to her car. The dog shook itself and padded after her, the tennis ball back in its mouth again. Barn didn't know whether to follow or not to explain why he had acted the way he had. Obviously he had scared her by his fast approach and the way he brushed past her, but it turned out to be a legitimate concern.

There were sharks.

More to the point, a shark had been scouting her dog.

The woman started her car and backed up harder than she needed to. The last thing Barn saw was the dog standing on the back seat, his head over the woman's shoulder.

He took out his phone and texted Lucas and Finn.

> Just saw a shark almost attack a dog. Def a bull.

F Crazy. Tomorrow we're on it.

Lucas texted a few seconds later.

L How big?

> Big enough. 6–8 feet maybe?

F Did you actually see the shark?

> Yep. Tell you later. TMT.

TMT. Too much to type.

He put his phone away. He looked at the water for a long

time, then climbed onto the Swagtron. He had to tell someone what he had seen. But who? His mom, sure. The police?
They weren't equipped to deal with sharks in a canal. People
knew about the attack—news cameras had been here just a
day before—but he doubted they recognized the danger
still swimming right beside them. The woman with the dog
sure didn't.

He felt the sun burning him into a potato chip. He kicked
the engine to life, but the battery had lost some of its pep. It
propelled the bike along, but not enough to get the air moving around him and not enough to shake the image of the
shark right behind the dog, its mouth starting to open.

Barn sat shirtless beside the kitchen table and let his mother rub aloe extract on his skin. It made him feel like a baby to let her do it, but it also felt great, soothing his raw back. The aloe came out of a squat bottle from Holly's Universal Galactic. His mother always had a vat of aloe around. And he always needed it. It took some of the sunburn away and made him feel cool and soft.

When she finished, she patted his shoulder and told him to put his shirt back on.

"Did you use sunblock at all?" she asked, screwing the top on the bottle of aloe.

"Some," he said, which wasn't quite the truth and wasn't entirely a lie.

"You are fair complected, Barn. You can't live down here and not use sunblock. How many times do I have to tell you?"

"I know. Sorry, Mom."

"There are real consequences for getting too much sun, Barn. Especially for a redhead."

"I know, Mom. I'll do better."

"When I see you burn like this, I wonder if we wouldn't be better back in Pennsylvania. I really do."

"I'm fine, Mom."

She kissed his cheek and went to the pantry to put the aloe away. He pulled on his shirt. He understood she wasn't serious about returning to Pennsylvania. The weather up north was horrible, for one thing, and they had been spoiled by the Florida sun for too long to go back to six months of winter. Besides, Pennsylvania held sad memories, memories of Barn's dad, the news of his death in Afghanistan, the feeling of collapse that came afterward. They had accepted Aunt Jupiter's invitation to come south and make a new start. It was better to be in Florida. She knew it and he knew it, but sometimes she needed to send out a ping like a bat checking its surroundings.

Except for the sunburn, he felt great. It had been an epic day. Things could change so quickly. He'd woken thinking all he wanted to do in the world was to watch the Red Sox at spring training; then the shark attack information came across his phone and away he went in an entirely different direction.

To top it off, he had gained seventy-two viewers at his phoebe nest cam. It was his most successful webcam exhibit ever.

"Will you set the table, Barn?" his mom asked when she came back to the kitchen. "Holly is going to join us."

"Okay. What's for dinner?"

"I made a salad. Holly's bringing some fresh shrimp and we'll put that on top. How does that sound?"

"Great."

He put out big, colorful striped bowls, the kind his mom liked to use for salads. And he added cloth napkins—they always used cloth napkins when Holly came over—and salt and pepper and water glasses and silverware. He was still setting the table when Holly knocked on the door, then came in, her tiny West Highland white terrier named Kong leading the way.

"Greetings to the house!" Holly called, which was what she always said when she entered a house. It was an Irish greeting of some sort, Barn knew.

"Greetings to Holly," his mom called back while Barn squatted down to pet Kong.

His mom and Holly hugged. Barn sat on the floor and invited Kong onto his lap. Kong was a great dog, friendly and smart, with tufted eyebrows. Sometimes they got to dog-sit Kong when Holly had to travel. He kissed Kong and petted him. Kong butted him softly with his head to keep Barn's attention. Meanwhile, his mom and Holly had the world's longest hug. They always did.

When they broke apart, Holly insisted that Barn get off the floor and hug her, too.

"You can play with Kong the rest of the night, but first you need to give your aunt Holly a hug."

He knew it was useless to protest. Holly hugged him hard. She smelled like citrus and Thanksgiving mixed together.

She moved him to arm's length while his mom began washing the shrimp.

"Did you go out in the sun without sunblock?" she asked.

"Not really . . ."

"That was aloe I smelled on you. Did you use the—"

"Aloe Ha Ha Bath," his mom said, speaking over her shoulder. "Yep. It's great stuff."

"The sun is our friend, Barn, but not in excess," Holly said. "Respect the sun. Especially the Florida sun."

Barn nodded and promised to do better, then he grabbed Kong and picked him up and headed to his bedroom. He usually took off with Kong until dinner.

He lay down on his bed for a while with Kong. What was great about Kong was the dog's ability to adapt himself to the mood of whomever he was with. Kong stood on Barn's belly, staring down at him. Barn stared back. It was pretty funny. Then Barn took Kong's front paws and pretended like Kong was dancing. Kong let him do it, all the while trying to maintain his balance.

"You are a good dog," Barn said, spacing out the words so that each part of the phrase was separate. "A very very very very good dog."

Kong kept looking at him, waiting for the next thing to happen.

They were still staring at each other when his computer dinged.

He carried Kong over to his desk and clicked on the video phone app. Finn slowly came into view. He sat too close to the camera, so that his entire face blobbed forward. Finn had dark, straight hair and a heavy brow ridge. He was adopted, Barn knew, from Greenland by a pair of physicians who had first encountered the Inuit population on a Doctors Without Borders mission.

"I'm back!" Finn said, his voice husky as it usually was. "I'll never go to Tennessee again."

"You had a bad time?"

Finn looked away, then looked back, checking to see if he could be overheard.

"It's soooooo boring. All anyone does is sit around and talk about whose relative did this or that."

"Was it a reunion?"

"No, it was just a reason to get together. I don't know. My mom kept saying it was about the importance of family. I must have watched fifty movies."

Finn loved movies. They both did, but Finn loved them more.

"Well, we can go over to the canal first thing tomorrow. Want me to pick you up?"

"Sure. I've got some ideas on what we can do."

"Cool. And remember Grandpa Lemon—"

"Wants me to fix his steering column. Yep, no problem."

Finn leaned closer to the camera. Sometimes Barn wondered if Finn's eyes were weak or something. He seemed to need to be close to things to see them properly.

"When I got back I told my mom about the shark coming after that dog and she called the police," Barn said, his hand running down Kong's furry back. "But they said they already knew about it and all the right people had been contacted. I don't think they understand what might be happening over there."

"People don't listen to kids, anyway."

"I know, but it was my mom. They kind of hustled her off like they had received a hundred phone calls and didn't care about one more."

"Well, you made the report at least."

"Yes, but someone could get hurt. They don't seem to be taking it seriously enough."

A few minutes later, his mom called him to dinner.

"Have to go," he said to Finn. "See you tomorrow morning."

"This is going to be awesome."

"It's intense."

"You going to any spring training games?"

"Not until this is over."

Barn clicked off. The phoebe cam had captured two more people's attention. He made Kong high-five him, then headed to the kitchen for dinner.

8

It was a little like a dream.

Barn saw someone standing at the foot of Finn's driveway, but it wasn't Finn. Barn squinted as he rode closer, trying to see who it was, because his initial impression was too unimaginable to believe.

It looked like Margaret Valley. It looked exactly like her.

But that didn't make any sense. For a moment Barn believed something about the strong morning sun had caused the optical illusion of making Finn look like Margaret Valley in his own driveway. That was just weird. Finn did not resemble Margaret Valley in even the slightest aspect, but to imagine that Margaret Valley herself stood at the bottom of Finn's driveway was simply unfathomable.

Two hundred yards away, he still couldn't say for sure.

One hundred yards away, the glimmering shape turned indisputably into Margaret Valley.

She sat on a bike. She wore shorts and a pink top and a wide straw hat with a navy ribbon around the top part. She wore canvas-colored Chuck Taylor Converse sneakers. She always looked like a picnic was about to happen or like she was about to jump on a boat. She had sharp, bony elbows and knees and her feet were usually dirty, because, she said, she liked to garden. Only the straw hat threw him. It wasn't something she typically wore, not that he knew about, and it seemed to soften her in a way he didn't fully understand. It framed her face, that's what it was, and he liked the way her eyes looked with all that straw in a halo around her head.

Barn slowed the Swagtron. Even now that he recognized her, it didn't add up. What was Margaret Valley doing at Finn's house? And why hadn't Finn told him what was going on?

But he couldn't slow down forever. It would look too obvious. He goosed the engine gently and kept going until he arrived at Finn's driveway. It connected to a huge house, Finn's house, financed by Finn's pair of physician parents. The house overlooked the sea. Finn's parents were rich.

Barn turned off the Swagtron and put his feet down on both sides of the bike. He tried to think of something to say to Margaret, but a frog had climbed into his throat. He couldn't think of a way to get it out.

"My parents are friends with Finn's parents and they had to go away for the day," Margaret said.

"Oh, I see."

"So they thought . . ."

Barn nodded. He could nod better than he could speak. He also became intensely aware of how random he looked. He wore the bandana under the back of his Red Sox hat and a bunch of white sunblock on his cheeks and forehead. He must have looked like a beach-going rooster.

Finally Finn appeared. He came down the driveway on his Dead Days Pintail Longboard, a huge red backpack on his shoulders. The way they usually traveled together was simple: Barn used the Swagtron and towed Finn on the longboard behind him. On downhills, they both coasted. Finn loved his longboard and

Barn loved his Swagtron. The combination worked.

But Margaret Valley was a wild card.

And she wore a straw hat that made her look . . .

He couldn't even form a thought about how she looked. She seemed embarrassed to be inserted into their plans. Barn couldn't tell if she had started to blush, too, or if the sun had already started cooking her. Either way, she looked great.

"Margaret's coming with us," Finn announced, hopping off the longboard. He snapped the ball of his foot against the back of the board and the board popped into his hands. "Her folks are busy or something."

"I can ride," she said. "I can keep up."

"We can all ride," Barn said, calculating. He was good at planning. That was one of his best skills. "Maybe take turns with the Swagtron."

"It's under ten miles," Finn said. "Piece of cake."

"You have all your stuff?" Barn asked.

Finn nodded. He jammed the backpack onto the back of Barn's bike and bungeed it in place. That's what they always did. Margaret watched. Barn kept his eyes down, concentrating on the job more strictly than he needed to do. *Margaret Valley*. He was going to spend the day with Margaret Valley. It still hadn't sunk in. He wondered if it would ever sink it.

"Good," Finn said when he had the bag secured. "Let's roll."

"You think the Swagtron can pull all of us?" Barn asked.

"If we can charge the battery at Grandpa Lemon's we can probably make it," Finn said.

It took a second to arrange. Barn tied a tow rope to Margaret's handlebars, and Finn tied a rope to the back of her bike. They looked ridiculous strung out in a straight line, he knew, but at least they could travel faster. Margaret seemed to be into it. She went along with everything and made two good suggestions about attaching the ropes. It was easy.

"Ready?" Barn called. "We have to pedal first, Margaret, then it will kick in."

"Okay."

"Ready, Finn?" Barn called a second time.

"Ready," Finn answered.

Barn pushed the pedal down. The rope sagged for a

second until he kicked on the engine. The rope snapped a bit as it drew tighter, but Margaret intelligently sped up to ease the pressure. Finally he felt them roll into a caravan, freight train mode. Finn let out a yell. And so did Margaret.

A smaller bull shark, one only slightly more than four feet in length, entered the southeastern tip of the canal from the bay on the high tide. It followed the shape and pull of the canal water, because its experience told it that the high tide brought food from the edges of the shoreline. Its senses pulsed with sharp, quick readouts. It had eaten once earlier in the day—two desiccated crabs near the Route 17 bridge that some fisherman had tossed into the water—but the crabs had only solidified its hunger.

The shells of the crabs could not pass through the shark's pyloric valve—the connection between the shark's stomach and its duodenum and valvular intestine—so the immature bull shark had already vomited the shells back into the sea. The rest of the crab's meaty parts had been dissolved by gastric acids and pepsinogen into a pulpy mush that oozed into the lower intestines. The shark's intestine had a spiral shape, scrowlike, that added surface area to the intestine to enhance digestion. It was a system that had changed little in more than a million years.

Now the shark required food, again. Its eyes, its nose, its lateral line all worked together to penetrate the water around it. It sensed the water becoming warmer and calmer, and it moved languidly up the center of the canal, three feet above the bottom. It did not waste energy. It swam only as much as needed and only at a speed sufficient to keep its senses panning the water for traces of food. It would eat dead or live things, fish or mammal, even crustaceans.

A quarter mile into the canal it picked up a splash. The shark could differentiate between the casual sounds that water made and the uneven splashing of an animal traveling through the water. Its lateral line began to send messages to its brain. Its nose began moving back and forth, looking for clues to explain the movement of water.

Thirty yards up the canal, it saw the source of the splashing. Tiny white ripples dotted the surface. The shark moved upward through the water column, its body sensing the increased heat of the upper water, its eyes pinched by increased sunlight. It closed on the object, not sure what it intended. Hunger rested like a fist in its upper gut.

Its pectoral fins balanced its body, cleaving the water and monitoring the shark's yaw.

It had discovered a raft, a rubber raft, and the splashing motion came from hands and feet kicking and splashing on either side of the flat surface. The shark moved more quickly up through the water column. The splashing had stopped. Now the raft rested like a sheet of wood, bobbing slightly on the pull and push of canal water.

Five feet from the raft, the shark slowed. It did not smell food. It did not see food. But the hunger in its gut drove it forward and it hit the center of the raft with its nose. In the same instant, it turned away, diving back down in case the object had been a threat. Then it circled and came back up to the vicinity of the raft, confused and uncertain of what to do next.

The splashes on either side of the raft became more penetrating and faster. The raft began to move toward the side of the canal. The shark glided beneath it, its senses recording every movement, its hunger making it reckless.

9

Finn untied his backpack and put it on the hot asphalt of the street. Barn unscrewed a carburetor clamp from the bike frame and removed the Swagtron's battery. The battery had barely made it on a single charge to Grandpa Lemon's house. Pulling two people taxed it heavily. If Grandpa Lemon didn't let them charge the battery, or if they missed him, then it would be a long pedal home.

"Do you want me to lock the bikes with my chain?" Margaret asked, unwrapping a chain lock from the seat stem of her bike. "I've got one that will fit both."

"Yeah, do that," Finn said, his hands pawing through his backpack to check his tools. "Barn has a bad habit of leaving his bike unlocked. I always tell him it's going to get stolen that way."

"I trust people," Barn said.

It's what he always said.

"I don't trust people," Margaret said, her hands lacing the bike chain through the center frames of both bikes and hugging it around the telephone pole. "When I was a little kid, someone stole my favorite toy. One of my friends! It turned me sour on all of humanity."

It was a joke. Barn looked at her. He had never heard her joke before. In school, they didn't spend a ton of time together. He smiled. Finn nodded and kept digging through his bag.

"Whenever you're ready," Barn said. "If the guy's around, he'll be out on his boat."

"Old guys always have some sort of project going on. It's what they do," Finn said, hoisting the bag. "Let's do it."

Barn led the way. He had already explained the situation with the steering column to Margaret and she had understood immediately. He had to pick his path in the opposite way down past two houses to get a passage to the canal walkway. Then he led them back along the canal walk, reminding them to be careful. The sun boiled everything it touched, even though it was merely mid-morning.

Grandpa Lemon stood on his boat talking to a young man, maybe mid-twenties, Barn guessed. They both stood in the shade cast by the boat's cuddy, the small cabin attached to the deck. The young man had long hair and a bunch of tattoos everywhere. He wore frayed shorts and a sleeveless T-shirt. He had long fingers, too, that Barn thought would be good for tying fishing flies or something delicate. He looked a little ragged. The faded print on his shirt said CRABBY JOE'S BAR AND GRILL.

"There they are!" Grandpa Lemon said when he spotted them approaching.

Barn suspected Grandpa Lemon had greeted them enthusiastically because the tattoo guy had too much to say. Grandpa Lemon turned to them and that got the tattoo fellow to stop talking.

"Is this your friend?" Grandpa Lemon asked, putting his hand up as a visor to his eyes.

Barn introduced Finn and then Margaret.

"And this is . . ." Grandpa Lemon said, but he didn't seem to know the tattoo guy's name.

"Lenny," Lenny said.

"He was just telling me he thinks he got bumped by a shark. He was on a rubber raft."

"I don't think I was bumped," Lenny said, raising his long fingers for emphasis. "I *was* bumped."

"Did you see the shark?" Barn asked.

"I saw the shark flash down afterward," Lenny said. "I mean, I saw the tail sort of behind it. I swear it followed me into the dock. When I climbed off the raft, it all felt sharky as anything. I swear."

Barn nodded. Whenever someone swore to something repeatedly, he believed them less each time, but Barn figured maybe Lenny was excited and couldn't help repeating himself. Meanwhile, Finn climbed on board the boat. His backpack made him look like a secretive turtle going down the ladder.

"So you're the electrical genius," Grandpa Lemon said, and pointed to the steering column. "You ever work on one of these?"

"All the time," Finn said, setting his backpack down and shaking Grandpa Lemon's hand. "These things always get messed up. It shouldn't be a problem."

Barn climbed down into the boat. So did Margaret. Lenny ran his hand through his dark hair. He appeared to like having a new audience for his story.

"How hard did it hit you?" Margaret asked. "The shark, I mean."

"Not too hard. I think it was testing. You heard about the kid who got chomped here, right?"

Margaret nodded. Barn did, too. The fact that someone got attacked by a shark nearby seemed to give Lenny confidence in his story. Maybe this was the most exciting thing to happen to him in a long while.

"I was sleeping, you know? When I woke up I had drifted up the canal. I started paddling a little. I guess the tide changed while I was asleep."

"It's going out," Grandpa Lemon said, breaking his conversation with Finn for a second to fill in the needed information. Old guys with boats, Barn knew, always tracked the tide. That's all Grandpa Lemon said, then he bent back over the steering column with Finn.

"So anyway," Lenny went on, "something hit me pretty hard from below. Right in the center of the raft. It was like a punch to the stomach, I swear. For a second I thought I had paddled onto something, but then when I looked to my right side I saw a big fish swimming down. A big one. Then it came back up and that's when I started paddling hard for the side of the canal."

"Any guess at length?" Barn asked.

Barn moved so he could get into the shade of the cuddy. The sun had already turned him into a lobster. Margaret moved, too. Before Lenny could answer, Barn heard Grandpa Lemon say, "Ooooh, yep, yep, I see it." Finn had just explained something to him. The old man bent hard over the steering column.

"Four feet or so," Lenny said, his eyes going back and forth from the steering column to Barn and Margaret. "Water makes things look smaller, you know? So maybe six. Probably six."

"What color?" Margaret asked.

Barn was impressed. It's the same question he had.

"Gray. Aren't most sharks gray?" Lenny asked.

"Most are," Barn agreed. "Not all, but most."

"Do you think it was a bull?" Margaret asked Barn.

Barn nodded, his heart beating fast at hearing the story. It was amazing. He was sure Lenny had experienced a bump. He was lucky he didn't go off the raft.

"Absolutely," Barn said, trying to control his excitement and his voice. "That would be my guess. They're aggressive. They check things out with their cheeks and mouth. It might have been testing to see if you were food. Lots of time, they can't see as well as they should, especially in murky water. They need to get up close to something to figure out what it is."

Lenny nodded hard. Apparently Barn had confirmed something that Grandpa Lemon had been reluctant to concede.

"That's what I figured!" Lenny said, his voice rising. "Gramps here wasn't buying it, but I told him."

"I bought it," Grandpa Lemon said, apparently able to track two conversations at once.

Finn stopped for a second. He had been twisting something with a pair of needle-nose pliers. Barn had seen him stop in the middle of a repair a thousand times. Finn had a chart of the circuitry in his head and he had stopped to refer to it. That's what made him a genius at that stuff.

"I'm going to tell the committee what happened," Lenny said. "They should be shutting this place down."

"What committee?" asked Barn.

"They've called a community meeting," Grandpa Lemon said. "Tomorrow night in the community rec center. Everyone along the canal is invited. They'll have some people from Fish and Game, too. I don't know what all. Someone reported seeing a dog almost get attacked."

"That was me!" Barn said, feeling his face blush. "I called that in."

"Well, glad you did, because it got some action."

"They should shut the canal down," Lenny said emphatically.

"No one's going to shut it down," Grandpa Lemon snapped. "That's foolishness. You have more chance of being struck by electricity than you do being bitten by a shark."

"But maybe not in these waters," Margaret said. "Maybe these are special conditions."

No one said anything to that. Lenny climbed off the boat and put his hand to his eyes to protect them from the sun.

"Someone else is going to get killed around here," Lenny said. "You wait and see. They should set off some explosive charges or something up and down the canal. They really should. It's sharks or us."

"That's ridiculous," Barn whispered.

Barn didn't speak again until Lenny had walked away.

"What's ridiculous?" Margaret asked.

"Bombing sharks. Killing them. That's not the right way to go about it. Sharks have as much right to be in the water as any other creature. Besides, an explosion might send them away for a brief time, but it's not the fix we need. It's not the answer."

Barn felt his heart still pounding. He loved sharks, but it was more than that. He loved nature and its balance. Who knew what it would do to the other creatures in the lagoon, the crabs and tarpon and snook?

"We need to get Fish and Game involved," Barn said.

He knew he had been living inside his head for a second. *Shark world*, his aunt Jupiter called it. He looked around as if he had just returned from a dream. Margaret smiled at him. Finn and Grandpa Lemon went back to fiddling with the steering wheel column.

Mrs. Grandpa Lemon served them lemonade on the boat
an hour after Lenny departed. She came out once to
check on her husband, met them all, and told them to
stay in the shade. Five minutes later she returned with
the lemonade. It was excellent lemonade. Barn drank a
glass straight down. So did Finn. Margaret drank a little
slower.

"My real name is Janet," Grandma Lemon said, pour-
ing more lemonade from a large, frosty pitcher. "Grandpa
Lemon isn't really his name. Our last name is Lennon, so
our youngest grandbaby confused the name and said
Lemon. So he's naturally calling himself Grandpa Lemon

now. He thinks he's funny. Most people call him Junior. Junior Lennon."

Grandpa Lemon fit him better, but Barn didn't want to point that out.

For a while, they drank lemonade and watched Finn work. When he worked, Finn concentrated like no one Barn had ever known. Even Grandpa Lemon stood back to watch. After a while, Janet went back inside. Barn asked her if he could plug in his battery charger. She showed him an outlet on the exterior of the house, maybe twenty feet from the lip of the canal, and he plugged it in. He hoped it would have sufficient time to charge. The sun poured itself over and over against the house. Barn didn't know if that would injure the battery. He hoped not. Finn would know.

By the time he made it back to the boat, Finn had finished the wiring.

"That should do it," he told Grandpa Lemon, wiping his hands on his shorts. "Let's fire her up and give her a try."

He screwed on the top portion of the steering column. He didn't tighten it down all the way. Grandpa Lemon appeared delighted. He started the engine. Barn smelled diesel. The motor made a deep, thrumming sound and the water bubbled behind them. Barn heard the hydraulics operating as they switched the steering wheel and rudder back and forth. Grandpa Lemon and Finn nodded at each other a half-dozen times.

"Let's rig up the Splash Drone," Margaret said after watching them go through their checks. "Let's get that ready."

Which was a good idea.

It had been Finn's idea to bring the Splash Drone. He had borrowed the equipment from a guy he knew, a friend of a friend for whom he had done some electrical work. The plan was to hover the Splash Drone over the canal, let it settle on the water, then adjust the camera. It could drift down the canal and they could get different angles. They could also make it lift from the water, move up or down the canal in either direction, then settle it back on the water. It was a great way to achieve maximum coverage. The whole camera feed beamed back to Finn's phone so they could watch and record live. Finn had brought two frozen fish heads, too, that he planned to use for bait.

Barn dug everything out of Finn's backpack. He set the fish to thaw on the tail of the boat.

Margaret set the Splash Drone on the deck and together they checked to make sure it was properly linked to Finn's phone. It sent out a strong picture. Barn didn't know if it would continue to do so once it was in the water.

The boat engine turned off.

"I am entirely impressed, young man!" Grandpa Lemon told Finn. "More than impressed. You don't find young people with your kind of skill every day."

Finn shrugged. Barn knew that repair jobs were easy for him. Barn had never seen him stumped by anything with circuitry. Grandpa Lemon took Finn inside to pay him. That left Barn and Margaret alone. He had never been alone with her for any length of time before and he felt super awkward.

"Think this will work?" Barn asked her because he had to ask something, say something. He was certain his skin was redder than tomato sauce from embarrassment and the sun.

"I guess. It's worth a try. It's fun to fool around with drones, anyway."

"Even if we see a bunch of sharks in here, I'm not sure what we can do about it. But as my aunt Jupiter says, you don't know what you can do until you know what you can do. I guess that's why we try."

She always said things like that.

Barn looked at Margaret. She seemed puzzled.

"Sorry," he said. "I get carried away sometimes. I mean, there *is* a danger here. We don't want anyone else to get hurt. If we can get proof that the sharks are here, visual confirmation, then whatever debate is going on will have more information. And we can help the sharks survive, too."

"That's true. It's not sharks versus humans. Everything is trying to survive."

"Right. So that's what we're doing."

It was easy to talk to her. Even for a rooster, it was easy. He liked being around her.

Ten minutes later, they had the Splash Drone set up and the first fish head tied to a separate rope, ready to dangle as bait. Finn and Grandpa Lemon had returned. Whatever came to feed on the fish head would be recorded by the Splash Drone. That, at least, was the working hypothesis. Even Grandpa Lemon liked the idea. He stood at the railing to his boat and watched them work.

"Are we okay?" Barn asked when they had everything ready. "Anybody see a problem?"

He looked around at them. They all shook their heads.

He tossed the fish head into the water and the line snaked after it.

"Do you think they'll go after it right away?" Margaret asked.

They all stood looking down at the line. The sun broke and refracted on everything it touched.

"I don't know," Barn said. "Depends on a bunch of things we can't control."

"My grandkids crab with fish heads," Grandpa Lemon said. "I guarantee there are plenty of those. Plenty of crabs."

Finn used a controller to get the drone to lift off. It hovered for a second like a dragonfly just above the boat, then Finn got it buzzing across the water, wobbling back and forth until he got the hang of flying it. Margaret held Finn's smartphone and described what she saw. Finn hovered the Splash Drone above the surface, approximately where the fish head had disappeared. Slowly he landed the drone on the surface. Its small glass bubble on the bottom made it float high in the water. Finn adjusted the camera.

"Have you ever been on a glass-bottomed boat? That's what it looks like," Margaret said.

"How's the feed?" Finn asked Margaret.

"Murky."

"Better now?"

He shifted something on the controller.

"A little, maybe. Not much. Point it straight down."

"I'm almost there now."

"I can't see anything but the sun bars going through the water. You know. Beams."

She had her eyes locked on the phone screen. Barn leaned over the edge of the boat and peered down into the water. He didn't doubt there were sharks. He didn't know *how many*. That was the question.

"That's pretty nifty," Grandpa Lemon said. "Darn, I could use one of those."

"A lot of fishermen are using them," Finn said, his eyes on the Splash Drone. "They can find schooling fish, big tunas, anything."

"Hardly seems fair to the fish."

"I agree," Margaret said.

Nothing happened. The sun beat them back into the

shade of the cuddy. It was midday, Barn knew, and probably not the best time to fish. Better to come at sunset. Better to fish in the middle of the night. But they needed light for the Splash Drone. They also couldn't be gone from home forever.

"Shouldn't we be hearing *Jaws* music by now?" Margaret asked. "You know: Duh duh. Dun duh dun duh dun duh dun duh."

That's when Barn felt the fish head line twitch. The line in the water began to go upstream, away from the natural flow of the water floating out toward the sea.

"Something has it," Barn whispered, his finger on the rope attached to the fish head. "Just lightly."

"Could be a crab," Grandpa Lemon said. "Could just be nibbling."

"Can you see anything on the feed?" Barn asked Margaret.

"No, nothing yet."

"Maybe if you raise it up. The fish head, I mean," Finn said. "Grandpa Lemon, how deep is the canal right here?"

"Twenty-five, thirty feet. Depends when they last dredged it. It fills in."

Barn felt something stronger move the fish head. They

had not put a hook in the fish head so the sense of *catching* a fish wasn't there. Whatever it was merely moved the fish along the bottom. Barn felt the line tightening across his hand. He raised his index finger to give the fish head some motion.

"I see something," Margaret said, her voice excited. "A fish."

She moved and held out the phone so they all could see. Barn had to swivel his head from side to side to get the light off the screen. But something definitely moved down by the end of the rope. He couldn't say what it was.

But it was big. And it had obviously found the bait.

"I'm going to lift the bait a little higher," Barn whispered. "Maybe we'll be able to see it better. Be ready."

He raised it a foot. The line quivered for a second, then went slack.

"Anything?" he asked Margaret.

Nothing happened for a ten count, then she spoke.

"There, there, there's something!" she said excitedly.

"I can't see it," Grandpa Lemon said.

"There it is," Finn said, his finger circling a spot on the screen. "I see it."

So did Barn. It wasn't a bull shark.

"It's a goliath fish," he announced. "Not a shark."

"How can you tell for sure?" Margaret asked. "I can barely see it."

"If it has to do with sharks or anything underwater, Barn knows," Finn said. "Trust me. He can tell what it is just by the way it swims."

A goliath fish was a big predator, as round as a log, with a mouth that spread across its entire body. It was a kind of grouper. This one wasn't huge, Barn didn't think, but they could grow to be enormous. He couldn't see it clearly.

"I'm going to raise the bait up a little more," Barn said, his eyes going back and forth from the line to the phone, then back again. "The goliath fish should have already taken it by now. I don't get it."

"Can you eat goliath fish?" Margaret asked.

"Sure," Grandpa Lemon said. "You can eat most any kind of fish. Some aren't worth eating, though. Almost anything out of the sea can be your dinner."

The goliath fish faded into the lower regions of the canal when Barn raised the fish head. Barn could tell that the goliath fish hadn't been eating the bait. It would have taken the entire head in one bite easily. Most likely, the goliath had come to check out the food. They could be cautious. You could dangle bait all day in front of a goliath and not catch one. On the other hand, you could get one as soon as the bait hit the water. Fish had their ways, Barn knew.

Then suddenly the line took off.

It took *off!*

Barn let it go ten feet, then he hauled back on it. Something big, something wild flew up the water channel. The water along the line bubbled and frothed, and Barn understood if he'd had a hook in the fish head it would have been time to reel in. Without the hook, though, the fish could simply spit the bait out unless it swallowed it first. Barn felt the force, the wild vigor of the fish in his hands.

Finn shot the drone off the water surface and repositioned it exactly on top of the fighting fish.

"It's a shark!" Margaret nearly yelled. "I can see it!"

"Look at that!" Grandpa Lemon said. "Christmas cookies, it's right there."

Barn forced himself to observe the shark, not merely respond to it. He concentrated on the blunt shape of the head. It was rounded and wide, but not long. He also decided it was a young specimen, because the tips of both the dorsal and caudal fins were dark tipped. The entire animal had a compact, sturdy body.

It was a bull. He didn't have a scintilla of doubt. Six feet, maybe.

The heavy line extended from its mouth like a piece of vertical spaghetti.

"It's a bull," Barn said. "Keep filming it."

"It's recording," Margaret said. "We've got it."

Then as suddenly as it started, the shark disappeared. The line popped free and all the tension that had been loaded a second before released. The canal surface calmed. Finn looked at Barn. Barn nodded. Finn lifted the Splash Drone from the water and brought it back to the boat.

"Confirmed sighting," Finn said, turning off the drone.

"Confirmed sighting," Barn agreed.

"That was AWESOME!" Margaret yelled.

And it *was* awesome. Barn had been so intent on observing the shark that he had almost lost sight of how amazing the whole thing had been. They had filmed a shark! They had proof of what was going on below the surface!

"Do your shark dance, Barn!" Finn shouted. "Do your dance!"

"No way!" he said, turning bright red.

"You have a shark dance?" Margaret asked, laughing. "Oh, I have to see this!"

Even Grandpa Lemon stared at him. Barn felt absurd.

But then Finn put his hand to his forehead, like a fin, and began dancing around. Completely goofy. So Barn took a deep gulp and did it, too. Margaret laughed and pointed at them both. Then Finn made her do it, too, and finally Grandpa Lemon shuffled around with his hand against his forehead. Barn couldn't help getting into it. It was so corny, so stupid, that for a second he forgot everything else and danced in the hot sun, a rooster shark, a redheaded bull shark, the worst dancing shark anyone had ever seen.

12

Aunt Jupiter met Barn at the door to his house. She held the screen door open, evidently on her way back out to her car to grab something, probably groceries.

"My favorite nephew!" she said in her big, gravelly voice.

Almost everything about Aunt Jupiter was big. He loved Aunt Jupiter more than any person in the world except his mom.

"Hello, aunty," he said.

He liked calling her aunty. Half the time she liked it and half the time she said it made her sound like an old lady with doilies and a dozen cats at home. She was his dad's sister. He understood part of their relationship had to do with the glimpse of her brother she could sometimes spot in him. That was okay with Barn. He liked hearing about his father from Aunt Jupiter. He loved the stories she told about them growing up in Pennsylvania. It brought his dad to life.

"I'm betting you forgot our date," Aunt Jupiter said, walking to her Jeep. "You did, didn't you?"

"I didn't forget it, exactly. I've just been distracted."

"Shark world?"

He nodded. It had been an amazing day. He didn't know where to begin to explain it all.

"Well, I've got our movie all cued up. Are you still up for it?"

"I am. Let me just get cleaned up. Then I'll tell you what happened. It was awesome, aunty!"

Margaret had said *awesome*. She was right.

"Come here first," Aunt Jupiter said.

She hugged him. Of all the hugs he received, from his mom, from Holly, the hugs from Aunt Jupiter were the most spectacular. Sometimes it felt like she might spring his ribs. She worked out all the time and she had played basketball for Lafayette College in Pennsylvania. She was as strong as an octopus.

"No Red Sox games this year?"

"Not yet."

"Don't let your Red Sox down, Barn. Sharks or no sharks, the Sox need you."

"I won't. Do you need a hand with anything?"

"Nope, I'll meet you inside. You are one burned tomato, kiddo. Your mother is going to make you stay in like a vampire when she gets ahold of you."

"I used sunblock. Honest. It's just . . ."

"Florida," she said, completing his sentence for him.

"Just Florida."

He went inside. He felt the sun slug him as soon as he stepped into the shade of the house. Working in the sun, doing things in the sun, you could sort of ignore it. But once you got into a place where the sun couldn't reach you, all the heat came back. Aunt Jupiter was right: His mom would kill him when she saw how much sunburn he had on his arms and face. He wondered, absently, if roosters got sunburn.

He went into the bathroom, washed, splashed a bunch of water on his face, then went to his room and checked to see if Finn's message with the shark video had arrived. They had looked at it on Finn's phone, of course, but Finn was going to work his miracle of enhancement to make the shark much more visible. Also, the Wi-Fi at the boat had been weak, so Finn had to send the full video when he got home. Now on the thread, Grandpa Lemon had written a note to tell them when the community meeting was being held concerning the canal.

And Margaret Valley had written, too.

He didn't want to read her message in one big gulp. He liked knowing it was there. It felt like the icing on a great cake of a day.

Aunt Jupiter had the shades drawn in his mother's office/den when he caught up to her.

"You ready?" she asked.

"You need to see this shark video first, aunty. I just got it. Finn cleaned it up, and it's awesome."

"Show me."

He did. He played it twice, each time catching a little more. Aunt Jupiter whistled after the second screening. Barn felt as if he were vibrating with excitement.

"You got that with a Splash Drone?"

"Finn did. But yeah. We worked together."

"And what are you going to do with it?"

Barn went through the entire story. He told her about the canal landowners' meeting the next night. He told her about calling the police after seeing a shark almost grab the dog in the canal.

"You're a pretty awesome kid," Aunt Jupiter said when he finished. "Really awesome."

"Thanks, aunty."

"Do you still feel like watching the movie? We don't have to."

"Of course I do. Let's do it."

He turned off his phone. She lifted a huge tin of caramel corn from the coffee table and set it between them. He gave her his full attention.

"Tonight's feature is *Double Indemnity*," she said. "Arguably the top noir film of all time. One of the top ten, anyway. You, my friend, are about to witness a miracle of cinema."

Aunt Jupiter loved movies. So did his dad. She said that was one of the things she always did with his dad, her brother. She claimed you should never feel guilty taking two hours out of your life to see something great. They had watched probably fifty movies together over the years. Most of her choices, though, were old movies, some black-and-white, that she figured he might miss if she didn't introduce them to him.

And she made the best caramel corn in the universe.

"Ready?" she asked.

"Ready."

"One, two, three."

They both roared like lions. It was something he had done as a little kid. When the lion for MGM films came on, he had roared back at the screen. Now they did it no matter what movie they watched. It wasn't a fake roar, either. They both roared as loud as they could. Then Aunt Jupiter pushed the play button and Barn reached for the caramel corn.

13

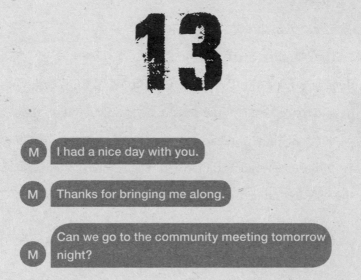

That's what Margaret wrote. He read the message in bed. He read it three times.

I had a nice day with you, he repeated under his breath.

What did that mean exactly?

He put his phone on his chest and tried to think of what

to write back. He definitely wanted to go to the community meeting and he definitely wanted Margaret to come, but the trick was to be enthusiastic . . .

. . . and warm . . .

. . . without being too idiotic.

I had, he wrote, then stopped. He erased it.

He put his phone back on his chest. He was sleepy, but not the nod-off kind of sleep he sometimes got on late school days. No, this was a slip-into-a-bathtub kind of sleepiness. All his chores were done. He had watched a terrific movie with Aunt Jupiter. And his mom had been sympathetic about his sunburn, but she recommended he at least take the morning off to let his skin recover. He asked if she would drive him over to Sarasota to get a second battery for the Swagtron. It was spending the morning in the shade, so he figured he had a shot. She said as a matter of fact she had some things to pick up, too.

Done deal.

I had a nice day with you.

He found that astonishing. Flabbergasting. Not that it wasn't a cool day. It was just that he didn't know she would like that sort of thing.

I had a smashing day with you, he wrote, then deleted it as fast as his fingers would move.

Smashing? Had he really written smashing? Did he think he was in one of Aunt Jupiter's old movies or something?

> It was great to hang out with you outside of school.

> Let's definitely go to the community meeting.

> We'll figure out details tomorrow, okay?

He read it, felt himself about to fall asleep, then read it again.

In desperation, he hit send.

Delivered, it said.

The little piano key marks next to the message started moving, indicating that she was writing back to him. He put the phone on the side of his leg, as if it were on fire. A second later the phone dinged that it had a new message.

Margaret's text popped onto his phone. She'd sent pictures. One of Grandpa and Grandma Lemon. One of Finn and Barn leaning over the side of the boat. One of Finn flying the drone. And one of herself, taken he didn't know when, standing between Finn and Barn. It was a selfie, but also a candid group shot.

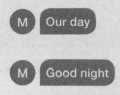

Good night

He forced himself to leave it at that. He turned off his phone. He was too tired. Sometimes when he spent too much time online he felt like he had shrunk down to an electric impulse and had drained into the wires, a tiny creature running back and forth from who knows where to who knows where. He closed his eyes and pictured the shark swimming. The one he had seen today. *Like bands of gray elastic*, he thought. Like a knife thrown through the water at a target somewhere out of sight.

"It's not a date. It's nothing like that."

"I know. I understand. I get it."

"I know, but I see your eyes getting all goony."

"Barn, I'm your mother. I'm the last person in the world you need to worry about."

"I'm not worried. I just want to be clear about things."

"Oh, I'm clear."

"See? Even saying that makes it sound weird. We're just going to the community meeting. Finn, Margaret, and me. We're going to see what people are going to propose about the sharks in the canal. That's it."

"Gotcha."

It drove him mad to listen to his mother's tone of voice. He knew if he had been in a court of law his mother would have been guilty of absolutely nothing. Zero. Nada. But something in her eyes twinkled when he said he wondered if she could give them a ride to the meeting.

Who? she had asked.

Finn.

Anyone else?

And Margaret Valley.

Then she had nodded and concentrated on driving their old Subaru wagon over to Finn's house because Margaret was still staying there.

It was 5:37. The sun was getting tired. Traffic was snarly. Barn found a Red Sox game on the radio. He reached over and turned up the volume. Everything considered, they had had a good day together. The mall in Sarasota had been fun, honestly, and his mom had been in a good vacation mood. She had shopped for clothes while he had gone to Home Depot to buy a battery for the Swagtron, and then they had eaten Korean food at the Bann Restaurant. His mother had been happy to spend the day with him, and he was glad to be with her, but when Finn and Margaret texted, asking if his mom could drive to the meeting, that's when things had gotten a tiny bit weird.

Mom weird.

Luckily, the conversation was cut short as they pulled up Finn's driveway. Finn and Margaret stood outside. Margaret had a yo-yo. She was showing Finn a trick of some sort.

"Hi, Finn, hi, Margaret," his mom said when they opened the back door to get in. "Nice to see you both."

"Hey," Barn said.

"Hello, Mrs. Whimbril," Margaret said, sliding in.

She wore a fleece and jeans. Finn wore his gray hoodie with the word *naatsiliat* printed on the front and back. It meant "potato," or "one who waited to grow," in the Inuit dialect of south Greenland.

"I dug around in the video and we have more to show you," Finn said, his voice rising in excitement. "There were at least three sharks. I had to tune up the contrast a mile. You have to know what you're looking for."

"Three," Margaret echoed.

"Amazing," Barn said. "Going after the bait?"

"Yep."

"And one was really big," Margaret said.

Then his mom asked for directions and Barn told her how to go. They made it in no time, but there didn't seem to be many cars parked in the small lot that circled the community building. Barn wondered if they had the wrong night, but then Margaret spotted Grandpa Lemon.

"Okay, I'm going to park out here and read while you guys do your thing," his mom said. "Remember, take it easy in there. You three are probably better informed than some of the people who will speak."

"We will," Barn said, wondering what that phrase—take it easy—even meant in this instance. "Thanks for the ride, Mom."

He touched her hand down by the seat. She squeezed his fingers.

"There you are! The shark squad!" Grandpa Lemon said when he saw them. He walked toward them—*waddled, really*, Barn thought. It was strange to see him at a location other than his boat. "The meeting has been delayed a half hour. I guess the traffic was bad and the Fish and Game people are running a little behind. I came over so you wouldn't think it had been canceled."

"We found two more sharks in the video," Finn said. "That place has a lot of sharks."

"One of them was big," Margaret added.

Finn showed them the video on his phone. It was startling. Three sharks had flashed at the bait. One—maybe eight feet, Barn guessed—chased the other two smaller sharks away. But it was a medium-sized shark that finally snapped the bait away. It was a little hard to see the action clearly, but Finn played it twice and the second time the events became clearer.

"That's unbelievably awesome," Barn said, amazed at how much Finn had been able to pull out of the murky video.

"Right outside my door," Grandpa Lemon said, then whistled lightly under his breath. "Wow. Who knew? This is going to shock a lot of people."

After that there wasn't much to do. Finn made Margaret take out her yo-yo. It turned out she was really good with it. Incredibly good. Grandpa Lemon loved the yo-yo and began talking about yo-yos he'd had as a boy, what they were like, and all the usual grandpa talk about the past, and America's youth, and questions about why kids don't play what anymore.

Barn watched Margaret walk the dog, rock the baby, shoot the moon, and couldn't believe how . . .

. . . adorable . . .

. . . cute she looked.

Finally people started to arrive. Two older people, a man and a woman, came on a tandem bike. A few pickup trucks came into the parking lot and backed up as if the drivers would have to run out of the building after the meeting and take off like firefighters. A small, stout man drove his Camry into the lot and stepped out and stretched his lower back. He reached inside his car and pulled out a green lanyard filled with keys.

"That's Don Wayland," Grandpa Lemon said, pointing with his chin. "He's the community selectman or whatever they're calling him these days. He's the one who called the meeting. He'll open the building."

Don Wayland wore an Aloha shirt with a bright blue background dotted with white palm trees. He jingled the keys and said hello to a few of the people milling around the door. They all turned when a green van with FLORIDA FISH AND GAME stenciled across the side pulled in beside one of the big Dodge pickups.

"Good, they're here," Don Wayland said, turning to open the door. "Let me get some AC on to cool off the building. Junior, would you go say hello to the Fish and Game people and bring them inside?"

It took a moment for Barn to remember that most people called Grandpa Lemon *Junior.*

"Come on, kids," Grandpa Lemon said. "Let's say hello."

Barn followed. Finn and Margaret went inside to see if it might be possible to hook up Finn's phone to an audiovisual display in the community building. Grandpa Lemon had doubted they had such an accommodation, but Finn said he might be able to figure something out. They disappeared into the rec center.

Only one person climbed out of the Fish and Game van. He was a tall, big man, maybe six three, with an enormous moustache and blue, happy eyes. The moustache made it look like he had not quite finished swallowing a broom. He had light brown hair, gray around the edges, and thick shoulders. His left arm from the elbow down was gone and in its place was a metal-and-plastic prosthetic. He wore thick boots that went up to his knees and a green Fish and Game shirt with his name in threads across the pocket: JESSUP SABINE. He also carried a half machete, about ten inches long, tied to his right leg. Barn couldn't help thinking it was cool to have the kind of job where you had to wear a machete to do your work properly. Inside the van, Barn spotted nets, a tree saw, and a canister of some chemical, and a bunch of work gloves. He also saw a dead possum on the passenger side floor and a bag of ice beside it.

"Welcome," Grandpa Lemon said, extending his hand. "I'm Junior and this is Barn."

Jessup Sabine smiled at them both but didn't saying anything. He held out his hand. Grandpa Lemon shook hands first, then Barn. Barn had never felt a heavier or harder hand.

"Jessup Sabine," Jessup said. "Here about that shark problem you all reported."

Jessup Sabine had the thickest, slowest Southern drawl Barn had ever heard. Each word weighed about fifty pounds, it felt like. Jessup Sabine had to lift the words one at a time.

That's what Barn thought, anyway.

"This young man and his friends have managed to film the sharks. They're trying to set up a video in the community center to show the members."

"You don't say," Jessup said.

Grandpa Lemon looked at Barn. Barn didn't know what to say. What did you say to someone who said you don't say?

"Bull sharks, I think," Barn said.

"Most likely," Jessup agreed. "That would be my first thought."

"Well, I guess we should get inside. There is some community concern. Pushback, you might say," Grandpa Lemon said.

"Always is," Jessup said, shutting the door to the van.

"Why do you have a dead possum?" Barn couldn't help asking.

"Dinner," Jessup said, and clicked the lock down.

15

The room filled by five minutes past the hour. The air-conditioning that Don Wayland had turned on couldn't keep up with the heat from so many bodies. Barn scanned the crowd and made a rough count. Forty people, maybe. Probably most of the homeowners along the canal.

After everyone had a chance to settle, Don Wayland walked to the front of the room and tapped his keys against a lectern set up there. People quieted quickly. Jessup Sabine stood back and to the right, almost like a bodyguard for Don Wayland. Barn saw Finn working on something to the left of the tiny stage at the head of the room. Barn figured Finn would get the video going. If he bothered to work on something, then most likely it would work.

"Ladies and gentlemen, thanks for coming this evening. If you don't mind, I'd like us to have a moment of silence for the young man who lost his life in our canal."

That made things serious. Finn stopped working. Barn looked around but couldn't see Margaret anywhere. During the moment of silence, he bowed his head and told himself not to sneak peeks at other people.

That was when he felt Margaret come to stand beside him.

When he looked up, she was there. He glanced at her. She smiled.

"Tonight we're meeting because we have a situation in the canal that is troubling, to say the least," Don Wayland began. He was already sweating, Barn observed. "I've asked the Florida Fish and Game Department to swing by and talk to us about possible causes and possible remedies. Right now, we need to keep the canal closed until we know what we're dealing with. It's all a bit unclear at the moment."

"You're the only who is unclear, Don," said a large man in a sleeveless T-shirt. The man had an enormous belly, a belly that folded over his belt, and a pelt of chest hair so thick it looked like an artificial putting green. "I didn't buy a house on this canal to have it shut off. If we need to dynamite this thing, then that's what we should do and no more talk about it."

A few people grumbled. A few more, maybe even the majority, made sounds like *hear hear.*

"Ladies and gentlemen, for those of you who may not know him, that's Ben Paio. He's contacted me several times about the situation we're facing. Ben, let's get the information first," Don said with surprising calm. "That's why we called this meeting."

"A boy got killed," a woman on the other side of the room said. "That's most of the information I need. I say we dynamite it. Or maybe poison."

Barn felt nervous and amazed. People got caught up in the moment. He knew that, but it was different to see it in action.

"I'd like to see the video . . . I'd like all of us to see this video made by these three young people just yesterday," Grandpa Lemon said, stepping forward and to one side of Don Wayland. "My friend Finn says he can play it over the old system right here. It's only a few minutes. It will show us what we're dealing with."

"We know what we're dealing with . . . ," the man in the T-shirt, Ben Paio, said again, but he was drowned out by people agreeing to watch the video. Everybody likes a movie, Barn realized. Grandpa Lemon nodded to Finn. Margaret worked her way to the door and flicked off the overhead lights. The video started.

"Whoa," a couple of people said when the sharks flashed at the bait.

More comments followed, most of them stepping on the one just before it.

"No wonder . . ."

"That poor kid."

"What are they going after . . . is that a fish head?"

"I let my kids swim . . ."

"We're going to get sued . . ."

The video was too short to create much more discussion. On his own, Don Wayland asked Finn to play it again. Finn did. This time people watched in silence.

"Yep, we have sharks," Ben Paio said. He had a tattoo on his arm that was as yellow as a dried egg. "Tell us something we don't know."

That's when Jessup Sabine stepped forward.

"You got bull sharks," he said when the lights came up.

He didn't say anything else for a moment, but everyone paid attention.

"My name is Dr. Jessup Sabine," he said when enough time had passed. His voice was so deep, his speaking voice so slow and filled with authority, that no one could think about interrupting. "I'm from the University of Florida originally and now I work with the Florida Fish and Game. What these young people have captured is a video of a good school of bull sharks patrolling these waters. Just so you people understand, the bull shark is the most aggressive shark we know about. All the big press clippings around the country are about great whites, as you know, but the day-to-day shark attack, the most fatal shark, I should say, is the bull shark. Hands down."

"But not as deadly as pet dogs," Barn couldn't help himself from adding, even though he knew he turned bright red when he spoke in public "And also less deadly than cattle. There are usually only five to fifteen shark attack fatalities around the world a year. Those are mostly due to more and more people swimming in coastal waters."

He had interrupted. He turned even redder.

"Sorry," he said. "I'm very into sharks."

A few people laughed. And someone even applauded. But the claps didn't catch on.

"The young man is correct," Jessup Sabine agreed, nodding in Barn's direction. "Dogs cause more deaths each year than sharks. So having sharks in your canal is not truly the issue. They have probably been here from the first moment the canal was connected to the bay. Having many sharks, and sharks of substantial size . . . that's the issue."

Almost comically, people turned to Barn as if he had something to add again. He shrugged.

"They're coming for food," Jessup said, continuing. "Just like animals come to a garbage dump. Or crows to roadkill. My first recommendation is to cease all fishing, all fish cleaning, all crabbing from the sides of the canal. As of this minute. I would also keep it posted against swimming for the foreseeable future. In a month or so, we could shock the canal and take a census. See where we stand. We'd probably have to close the canal to boat traffic for a day, but not much longer. You've got a problem here, but it's a human problem, not a shark problem."

The crowd buzzed. Margaret had worked her way beside him again. Finn had come over, too. He had just arrived when the big man in the T-shirt demanded everyone's attention.

"This is a safety issue, true," he said, speaking too loudly. "I get that. But it's also a real estate issue. We don't want our land values to go down because we have some sharks swimming in the canals outside our houses. There are sharks in every canal in this state, I bet. Alligators, too, and sometimes even pythons. Big snakes. I've seen them."

That got everyone murmuring. Barn wasn't sure the claim about snakes had merit. Florida had plenty of snakes in the Everglades, for sure, and most recently an influx of Burmese pythons that had grown to startling proportions, but it was unlikely that snakes proved any kind of a problem in Apple Way Canal. That didn't ring true, but something about the man speaking made Barn reluctant to contradict him. He seemed angry and frustrated and ready to argue with anything anyone said.

Ben Paio continued.

"I have a friend . . . I told him about our situation and he's a demolition expert. He said we could set up a string of charges here, very subtle, and bye-bye sharky. We don't need a bunch of environmental hoo-ha about nature. Probably five hundred dollars maximum and the problem is over by this weekend. That's my recommendation."

"That's what I'm talking about," the woman who had spoken earlier said. "That's it, Ben. You tell them."

"That would be against the law, for one thing," Jessup said calmly, "and it would be ineffective for the second thing. You might scare off and kill some sharks, but they'd come right back if there's a food source."

"Not if we do it once a month. My friend says that's the ticket," Ben said. "Like any kind of exterminator . . . ants, termites, cockroaches, what have you. You just stay on top of it."

Barn realized Ben Paio enjoyed this. He liked being in the public eye and he liked playing the tough guy. Barn didn't doubt he had a temper. At least that's how he seemed.

"Well, it sounds like it's not viable in any case if it's against the law," Don said, stepping forward again. "I move that we create a committee to study this further and to make a recommendation. We could do it in short order. Meanwhile, let's suspend all fishing and crabbing from the canal. Keep things clean. That can't hurt. Do we agree on that?"

People made noises. *It was hard to say what it meant,* Barn thought. Ben had a group around him and they seemed excited and defiant. Barn couldn't quite figure them out. They didn't want sharks in their canal, and they had been told by Jessup Sabine what do about it, at least the first step, and yet they wouldn't accept the information. Barn didn't understand why someone would invite a scientist, hear what he had to say, then dismiss it. It was like visiting the doctor and then telling her or him you knew better. It was goofy.

"All we're suggesting . . . ," Don Wayland said in a loud voice, tapping his keys on the lectern again to get everyone's attention. "All we're suggesting is we form a committee, a small committee, to look into the matter and make a recommendation. You are welcome on the committee, Ben. In fact, I invite you to be on it. Consider yourself nominated."

"I'd rather be a committee of one," Ben spoke back. "When you got squirrels in your soffits, you don't need a committee. I say we set some dynamite in the canal and talk about things afterward."

The room went silent. It wasn't that Ben had a great

grasp of the situation, Barn realized. He simply had the most emphatic point of view.

"Each year humans kill between twenty and one hundred million sharks," Barn said. He had started speaking before he knew he was going to speak. It was weird, but now that he had started he had to keep going. "If we can prevent killing a bunch of sharks here when there is another option . . ."

"Who is this kid, anyway?" the woman who seemed in league with Ben interrupted. Her voice was loud and sharp. "I don't want to be lectured to by a kid. Let's fix this now. I say dynamite."

Dy-na-mite!

Ben started chanting. It was meant to be funny, but in no time most of the people in the room had followed his lead. Barn looked around. He couldn't say if the people meant it or not, or if they were just caught up in the moment. Some of the people pointed at him, mocking. Barn didn't care what they said, but he knew that no one was going to listen to his point of view. He nodded and made his way to the back door. Margaret went with him. Finn said he had to get his phone from the audiovisual setup and would meet them outside.

Jessup Sabine reached the door at the same time as Barn and Margaret did.

"Well, you tried," Jessup said when they finally made it back outside. It was a warm night and the stars had just started to shake free of the darkness. "People hear what they want to hear."

"They're so rude!" Margaret said, clearly annoyed.

"People aren't much good in groups most of the time," Jessup said, his deep voice curling out into the night. "At least that's my experience. But you did a good job, both of you, presenting your case. People like the warm and fuzzy creatures. Bears and wolves and lions, but they have a hard time understanding it's all tied together. Nature is all tied together. It's a change of attitude we need toward animals, all animals, but I doubt that's going to start tonight right here."

"But what can we do? The sharks aren't doing anything wrong," Barn said. "It's not their fault."

He was surprised to hear his voice quaver. It was ridiculous how much he cared about sharks. He felt a little raw and mocked. It was like sunburn, only in his brain.

Jessup Sabine put his hand on Barn's shoulder.

"We'll ticket them if they go forward with the dynamite. I suspect that notion will blow over tonight. You can't start detonating dynamite charges in a residential area. It might even blow apart some of the canal and probably disable a boat or two. A lot of unintended consequences with dynamite."

"What, then?" Margaret asked.

Before Jessup could reply, a red pickup truck pulled into the parking lot and came to a stop right beside the door. A teenager jumped out of the driver's side and started toward the door. When he saw Jessup's uniform, he stopped suddenly and pointed to the back of his truck.

"I just caught a huge shark," he said, pointing and gesturing excitedly. "Right out here in the canal. I caught it from a kayak and it pulled me all over the place. You've got to see what I found when I gutted it."

Barn stepped to the back of the truck and looked down at the huge fish. He felt his heart get tangled inside his chest. *Carcharhinus leucas*, he whispered under his breath.

Bull shark.

Barn watched Jessup Sabine go to his truck and come back with a portable spotlight. He pointed it at the shark. The young fisherman leaned over the side of the truck. Jessup handed Barn the spotlight.

"Keep it pointed so I can see, okay?" Jessup asked. "Climb up and give me light where I need it."

Barn nodded and climbed into the truck bed. Finn and Margaret stood near the tailgate.

Jessup rolled the shark onto its back. He stood beside the bed of the pickup and used the flat surface of the truck as an operating table. He was tall enough to reach right in and do his work. He took a small piece of scrap wood he found in the pickup bed and pried it into place so that the cavity of the shark stayed open. It didn't bleed a lot. Barn had seen plenty of fish cleaned before, but he had never seen a shark of this size so close. The shark rested at his feet.

"It's almost nine feet," the fisherman said. "It's huge. I can't believe I even caught the thing. When I started to clean it, I saw . . . something. So I stopped. I came right over here. I didn't know what I should do. I tried to do the right thing."

Barn guessed its girth went about two or three feet, maybe more. It depended how you measured it. It had the pushed-in snout typical of a bull shark. Gray color, although it had already begun to lose its fresh appearance.

It was an enormous shark.

"Female," Jessup said, as if calling out the details on a TV medical show.

Barn admired his skill with the animal. Obviously, he filleted fish and other creatures often in his line of work. He knew what to look for and what to do.

"Females are bigger in bull sharks," Barn couldn't help himself from saying. "It's called sexual dimorphism."

Jessup looked up. He raised his eyebrows.

"I study sharks," Barn said. "Sorry."

"Nothing to be sorry about," Jessup said, going back to his work. "Go on. What else do you know?"

Barn didn't want to be a show-off, but it was surprising how few opportunities he actually had to talk about sharks. Really talk about them. He looked around the borders of the truck. People had wandered out from the meeting—it was stuffy inside and the same people kept talking over one another—and they didn't seem to mind hearing from him. In fact, they looked back and forth between him and Jessup's inspection of the shark.

"Well," Barn continued, "most sharks have the same salt content as the sea they swim in, but bull sharks function at fifty percent salinity. They have a different kidney function and they have corresponding glands in their tails to regulate their salt content. That's why they can travel into fresh or brackish water."

Barn stopped. He didn't want to be a know-it-all. To his surprise, the woman who had been an advocate of dynamiting the canal leaned forward through two men and spoke to him. She had joined the group around the truck.

"You keep going, honey. We want to hear," she said. "Tell us what you know."

Barn moved the light to keep it focused where Jessup needed it.

"It has around fifty rows of teeth in its jaws and each row has about seven teeth, making a grand total, give or take, of three hundred and fifty teeth. It may use twenty thousand teeth in its lifetime. It has the strongest bite of any shark species, relative to its body size. They can swim up to twenty-five miles per hour. They have placoid scales that overlap and make them streamlined for swimming."

"How long do they live, honey?" the woman asked.

"About fifteen years. They are requiem sharks, members of the genus *Carcharhinus* . . ."

And then he stopped talking. Because Jessup had finally uncovered what the fisherman had found—a pink flip-flop with a little rosette attached to the place where the two plastic bands joined above the toes.

"Holy . . . ," said the lady who asked questions.

"Is that . . . ," someone else started.

"You are not serious . . ."

"Oh, man . . ."

Jessup calmly slid the piece of wood away and closed the

cavity of the shark's body. He turned to the fisherman who had caught the shark from his kayak.

"I'm going to impound this fish," he said softly. "Sorry, but I think you understand. The shark has swallowed a flip-flop, but that doesn't mean anything necessarily. We find all sorts of things in sharks' bellies."

The young man nodded.

"You can have it," the fisherman said. "I sure as heck don't want it."

Everyone had gone silent. Barn moved the light away from the shark's body. He looked at Jessup, then looked at the other people around the bed of the truck. He saw shock in their expressions.

Only Ben Paio found his voice.

"Now maybe you'll listen to me," he said with his booming voice. "Maybe now you'll think about dynamiting this canal!"

17

"That's quite a knowledgeable boy you have," Jessup Sabine said to Jane Whimbril. He had just finished closing the door of the van on the bull shark. He turned around and there was Barn's mom.

Barn watched in dismay.

It was *awkward*.

"I heard you say you're a doctor," his mother said, and she seemed genuinely interested. She also hadn't brought her hand back to her side right away after shaking his hand. "What's your area of study?"

"Marine biology."

"Did you go to school around here?"

"University of Florida. I specialized in ground stocks. Cod, mackerel, that sort of thing off Georges Bank in Massachusetts. Then I became interested in algae and red tide growths, and that's when Florida Fish and Game asked me to come aboard. Been here about seven years."

They let go of their hands, but their eyes remained on each other. Barn watched and felt peculiar.

"And you?" Jessup asked with his fifty-pound words. "How do you keep body and soul together?"

"I'm a high school English teacher at Sarasota High. Ninth and tenth grade."

Jessup nodded.

"Will you finish the autopsy tonight?" Barn asked, mostly to get them to stop looking at each other. "Or wait until tomorrow?"

"Oh, tonight, I suppose while things are fresh. I'll call the police and ask them what they might have for missing persons. They'll want to get a medical examiner over. Could be just a flip-flop. We'll have to check the stomach more thoroughly. I didn't want to do it in a public space."

"It was shocking to see the flip-flop," Barn's mom said.

"When you think of what it could mean, it's horrible."

Jessup nodded. Barn did, too. That's where things stood until Jessup dug into his back pocket and came out with his wallet. He opened it and extracted a business card. Two business cards. He gave one to Barn, the other to his mother.

Which was awkward again.

"If you want to come by tomorrow morning we'll probably have the results," Jessup said. "We open shop at eight. Easy enough to find."

"At this address?" Barn's mom asked.

"At that address. And that's my personal number if you want to reach me."

He touched his finger on her card to point out his number. His mother, Barn noticed, cocked her head a little and smiled up at him.

"I'll bring him by at eight if you think that would be okay. I'm sure he'd like to see the lab work. Maybe he'll just ride over on his bike."

Jessup nodded again. Then he climbed into the van, started it, and drove off. His mom slipped Jessup's card into her back pocket. Barn wanted to say something—something about Jessup having a machete tied to his leg or something like that—but he couldn't form the words. He looked at his mom.

"What?" she asked.

He shrugged. Shrugs usually worked.

"What?"

He shrugged again.

Fortunately Grandpa Lemon came and said hello at that point. He had Finn and Margaret with him. Grandpa Lemon spent a little while saying how exemplary he found Barn and his friends. He told his mom at length about the repair of his electrical work. Barn watched his mom nod and agree. When she found a polite place to insert a word, she told Grandpa Lemon she needed to get everyone home.

"Fine, fine," Grandpa Lemon said. "They're welcome anytime. All of them. Wonderful kids."

"Thank you. I think so," Barn's mom said. "I think they're wonderful, too."

It was completely dark now except for the lights on the community center. A few bats flicked by overhead. Barn walked beside his mom to their car. Finn and Margaret climbed in the back. Barn felt his belly had slipped into a knot and wouldn't come undone.

"That flip-flop," Margaret said as the car started. "I had a pair exactly like those when I was little."

"It doesn't mean anyone was eaten," Finn said, fiddling with stuff in his pockets. "You can't go there right away."

"It doesn't mean anyone wasn't, either," Barn said.

"I think I would rather die just about any way in the world other than shark attack," Margaret said. "It's a terrifying idea to have something trying to drag you under."

"I'd go by a cougar bite if I had to die by a bite," Finn said, looking up, as if the death grip of different animals was a topic he often contemplated. "Blammo, they grab you right in the back of the neck and you're dead. It wouldn't take long. You wouldn't even see it coming."

"Believe it or not," Barn said, remembering an article Lucas had sent him, "a constrictor snake is supposed to be the fastest way to go. You get squeezed by a python and it's all over in under two minutes."

"This is a gruesome conversation," Barn's mom said, switching on the radio to National Public Radio. "Can we talk about something else, maybe? Or just listen to the news for a few minutes?"

Nobody else had much to say. Barn looked out the window and wondered about the flip-flop. He wondered about it a great deal. His mind had a lot of thoughts spinning through it.

18

Unconsciously, Barn twirled a few strands of hair with his index finger, his eyes locked to the screen of the iPad on his lap. Hair twirling was something he did without knowing it, something he did whenever he needed to concentrate. He did it when he was sleepy, too, or overtired, but he was anything but fatigued reading Dr. Jessup Sabine's forensic report.

But it was difficult language. Scientific language.

"So there was no evidence of a human being . . . ?" Barn asked, making sure he understood.

"No. We are fairly certain it was a false alarm. The flip-flop got us all going. They are going to test it again, but it doesn't look like there was a victim. Thank goodness."

Jessup had a bottle of green cleaner and a sponge. He cleaned the metal autopsy table or the dissection table or whatever it was called. He had his sleeves rolled up and he looked tired. He had been up all night. Barn had arrived at eight and had encountered four members of the county forensic team removing three vats of surgical materials. At least he had guessed they were filled with surgical materials. They had been sent off with the police lab people for further testing.

"Why did they take the material from the shark?" asked Barn, alternating between reading and watching Jessup.

"To be on the safe side. Just in case."

Jessup sprayed some more green cleaner on the table.

"That's intense," Barn said.

"That's one word for it."

"So it just ate the flip-flop? Maybe it was inside a bag it ate or something."

"Maybe. Or it may have mistaken it for something else. The silhouette might look like a turtle swimming. Who knows? It probably resisted digestion. What are flip-flops made of?"

"Beats me. Some kind of rubberized plastic, I guess."

"Maybe the point is we all thought it *could* be a victim. We have to keep that in mind."

Barn nodded and felt relieved that the flip-flop had proven to be a false alarm. He closed out of the file on the iPad and took a breath. It was awesome to be in Jessup Sabine's office and lab. It was a beautiful facility, with fresh grass outside and a small meditation fountain in the courtyard at the center of the building. Jessup was more important than Barn had realized the night before. Barn couldn't tell if there were ranks in the Fish and Game Department, but people seemed to defer to Jessup Sabine. He had three people working for him in outer offices, and a young grad student named Kelly had been there when Barn arrived. But Kelly had left with the rest of the forensic team, leaving Barn to sit and read while Jessup mopped up the mess from the night before.

"Where are your friends this morning?" Jessup asked as he wiped down the table. He cleaned the surface and the legs and the underside.

"They had to drive Margaret over to Fort Lauderdale. They'll be back this afternoon."

"I take it they're not as shark obsessed as you are."

"No, but I'm probably a little too crazy about sharks."

Jessup smiled. He kept cleaning.

"The truth is, sharks will scavenge just about anything You know the stories. We find license plates and wrenches and parts of automobile tires in their stomachs. They can digest almost anything, but not metal. Without that flip-flop, we never would have bothered to look any closer. That fisherman would have taken that shark home, filleted it, and tossed it away when he finished."

"Ben Paio is going to make this a big issue along the canal," Barn said. "He'll want to dynamite the canal more than ever. He'll say it could have been another victim."

"I only hope he doesn't take it into his own head to do that. Someone is likely to get hurt once people start playing with dynamite."

"I'm still wondering why the sharks are here at all," Barn said, going to help Jessup with the cleaning bucket. He poured it in the drain and then rinsed out the sink. "I mean, you have to separate the flip-flop in this shark's stomach and the situation with Robby White."

"The boy who was attacked?"

"Yes. It's easy to think they have to be linked, but really they aren't. Not by the sharks' eating patterns, but maybe by the canal."

"In other words," Jessup said, ducking to put the green cleaner under the sink, "one plus one doesn't necessarily equal two in this instance. I think you're correct. The shark with the flip-flop ended up in the canal, but that's independent of where the shark ate it. The shark came up the canal for other reasons. It wasn't hunting flip-flops. It was following scent and food, probably. Same goes for the shark that attacked . . ."

"Robby White," Barn said.

"Yes, Robby White. It wasn't in the canal to hunt for humans. It just saw an opportunity. You said the shark bumped him first, right?"

"According to the report."

"Well, so it probably tested the boy first. Tried to determine what it was sensing. When it didn't find any danger, well, then it launched its attack thinking it found food."

"We still need to find the thing that is drawing them up the canal. That's what you're saying, right?"

"I think it's the most likely explanation."

Barn nodded. They were on the same page.

"I guess I should get going," Barn said, remembering that his mom had told him not to overstay his welcome. "You've been up all night."

"I do need to sleep some. How did you get here? Did your mom bring you?"

"No, I have an electric bike. A Swagtron, and I can get around with that."

Jessup sat down on a stool near the dissection table. He motioned Barn to take a seat on the other side.

"Listen, I know you know sharks," Jessup said, "but you may not know sharks in the water. They are apex predators and you can't trifle with them. Especially bulls. They have nasty temperaments. I have to have your word you won't go in the water with them, try anything like that."

"I promise. My mom already made me promise."

"Your mom's a smart woman. Don't let your friends be tempted, either. Shark attacks are exceedingly rare, but sometimes circumstances make them more likely. Right now that canal is dangerous. We'll figure out what's happening, but right now . . ."

Barn nodded.

"You come by anytime you like," Jessup finished, rising. "I'm impressed by your shark studies. By your commitment to them."

"Thank you."

"I was a little bit like you when I was your age, to be honest. For me it was gators. I couldn't learn enough about gators."

He said *gators* in three syllables. *Ga-tttt-orrrs*.

Barn couldn't help it. He wondered if Jessup had lost his hand and forearm to a gator. He didn't dare ask.

He thanked Jessup, said goodbye, and walked out. He had parked the Swagtron in the shade of a camphor tree. He put his hand on the bicycle seat to see if the sun had made it hot, then he unlocked it and spent a minute fitting his helmet on his head.

Where to go?

He was equal distance from Apple Way Canal and home. It was still early in the morning, but he wasn't sure what he could accomplish by going to the canal. On the other hand, going home meant a longer trip back if he decided to return with Finn.

And maybe Margaret.

Without fully deciding which direction to take, he started up the Swagtron and climbed aboard. The sun had already found him and he felt its weight on his skin, his nose turning into a diving board for sweat.

19

Barn pulled up to the boat ramp on Apple Way Canal and turned off his Swagtron.

It was 10:07 in the morning and already hot as blazes. He quietly moved the bike over to the shade of a locust tree and stayed on the seat, watching the water. Although he had considered it, Barn didn't want to stop at Grandpa Lemon's house. He liked Grandpa Lemon, liked him a lot, but he didn't want to be tied to him on this particular day. Once he went to Grandpa Lemon's, that would be that.

Barn wanted to do some investigating, and he couldn't do that with Grandpa Lemon along.

He sat in the shade, not really thinking, but letting his

mind roam where it liked. It was a technique his aunt Jupiter had taught him. She called it woolgathering. She said sometimes you could think better by not thinking. That sounded strange, Barn knew, but he understood what she meant. Come at a thing sideways, in other words. Don't guide your thoughts, but let them find their way to your conscious mind.

So for a while, sitting in the shade and watching the peaceful water, he woolgathered.

Why would bull sharks come up a canal?

That was the central question. The only question, really. The answer had to be as easy as, *Why did the chicken cross the road?*

To get to the other side.

Why did bull sharks swim up a canal?

To eat. To hunt. To fill their bellies.

It was that simple. Somewhere, somehow, the bull sharks found the conditions ideal for hunting or eating or both. It had to be worth their energy to make the journey through the bay, then up the canal. In February, it was possible the sharks had entered the canal because it was warmer than the open sea. They could be mating, although bull sharks in southern latitudes could mate and give birth year-round. That probably ruled out mating as a cause.

It was food. Barn was pretty sure about that as an answer. Where did they find food?

He shook himself. He had almost dozed. He used his phone and sent a text to Finn and Margaret.

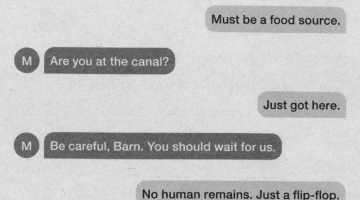

Must be a food source.

M Are you at the canal?

Just got here.

M Be careful, Barn. You should wait for us.

No human remains. Just a flip-flop.

No answer. Barn didn't know exactly what they were doing in Fort Lauderdale. It had something to do with Margaret's parents, who were not getting along, or having some problems. It wasn't any of his business until Margaret wanted to tell him about it. Barn almost let his mind go back to woolgathering when his phone pinged a new message.

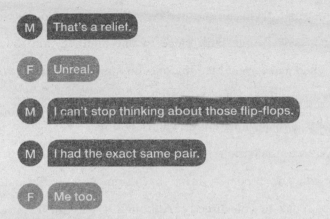

M That's a relief.

F Unreal.

M I can't stop thinking about those flip-flops.

M I had the exact same pair.

F Me too.

Finn meant it as a joke. Barn laughed.

Going to look around.

Must be a reason they come up the canal.

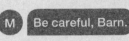

M Be careful, Barn.

It made him feel good that she wrote that. That she cared enough to write it.

He turned the handlebars and stepped on the pedals. It took him a second to get going up the slant of the boat ramp. When the road leveled out, he switched on the electric motor. It began to hum and push him along.

He drove slowly. He drove so slowly his bike nearly tottered over twice. Each time he realized he had been looking at the canal, trying to see it clearly through the houses. It wasn't easy. People built close to one another, and they often had fences, and that made seeing the canal and its two sides almost impossible.

He tried to clear his mind. He tried to *see*.

That was the trick to science. To discovery. You had to rid your mind of predetermined conclusions and let the evidence speak to you directly. Although it was fun to have Margaret and Finn along, he could concentrate better—*see* better!—investigating on his own.

He had gone nearly a mile when for the first time he saw what was obvious. It—they—were everywhere, but he hadn't noticed them before. He hadn't registered them in his mind. He turned around and went back over the same ground.

This time he looked for something specific.

He looked for solar panels.

The trouble—or not really trouble, but the flaw in his observation—was that people had solar panels everywhere. On their roofs, in their yards, on their docks. The surfaces of the solar panels glinted in the late morning sunshine like so many teeth grinning back at the sun. Solar power was a thing, that much was certain. People used it for everything. It made sense in Florida, perfect sense, but what Barn wondered about was the discharge of electricity into the water.

And he connected it to sharks.

Ampullae of Lorenzini.

Barn stopped and searched it on his phone to make sure he remembered it correctly.

Pores, located on the snout of a shark, ending in jelly-filled bulbs. The bulbs contain nerves to detect electric fields in the water as small as five millionths of a volt per centimeter. All ocean animals emit an electrical field, because muscle contractions release bioelectricity.

If solar panels, or wind turbines, or any sort of electric field bled into the water of the canal, the sharks might mistake it for food.

At least it served as a working hypothesis.

He drove three miles up the western side of the canal. Eventually the canal narrowed into a small, muddy gulley, devoid of houses. He turned around and drove back the way he had come until he found a footbridge that crossed from one side of the canal to the other. He turned off the engine when he reached the top of the bridge's arc. For a long time, even in full sunlight, he stared down at the water. He didn't know what he hoped to see. Sharks high-fiving each other? Sharks drawing up blackboard plans for an invasion?

He took out his phone and called Jessup Sabine.

No answer. After five rings Jessup's voice came on. Barn couldn't help smiling. With his Southern drawl, it took a long time for Jessup to say hello, give instructions for leaving a message, and to say goodbye. By the time he finally heard the beep, Barn felt silly bothering a PhD in marine biology. But he had to say something.

"Ampullae of Lorenzini . . . ," he began, then wasn't sure what he wanted to say. "I'm at the canal and I'm seeing all these solar panels. I don't know. It just seemed . . . maybe bioelectrical . . . that the discharge of the solar panels is being mistaken for a bioelectrical charge . . . Anyway, I'm looking to see what I can . . . see, I guess. Sorry if I am disturbing you. I just thought the sharks could be drawn up the canal . . . maybe it's a silly idea. Okay, sorry."

He sounded completely and utterly idiotic. That's what he felt like when he slipped his phone back in his pocket. His skin had turned red in embarrassment. He wished he had never called. Jessup Sabine would think he was trying to be a know-it-all, or a nuisance, or something unsavory. Besides, it really was a long-shot hypothesis. At best, he imagined, electrical impulses could be a factor in the situation. It didn't warrant a phone call to a biologist at Florida Fish and Game.

He took a deep breath. He put his feet on his pedals and pointed the bike down the far side of the footbridge. He had only gone a few feet when he smelled it.

Hamburgers.

He realized he hadn't eaten much all day. The smell of the hamburgers interlaced with fish smells and deep-frying potatoes caught his attention. He turned his head this and that way to get the location locked in. He used his own ampullae of Lorenzini. He clicked on the bike's motor and headed toward the smell.

20

Barn almost wanted to rub his eyes.

The Restaurant Restaurant.

It was supposed to be funny. Or hip. Or something. Barn couldn't tell. A vintage surfboard with the name printed on the top surface hung above the door. The restaurant looked like a thousand other restaurants in Florida. Gray wood and a gravel parking lot. It even had fishnets draped across the front of the building. It was a meta restaurant. That's what his mom, the English teacher, would have said. A restaurant that is aware of itself being a restaurant.

Barn locked the Swagtron to a parking sign in the shade of a loblolly pine tree. He realized he locked his bike more

162

often now that he hung around with Margaret. He wasn't certain the Restaurant Restaurant was open. Only three cars sat in the parking lot. He waited for a second in the shade, trying to assess the situation. He figured it wouldn't hurt to try it. And the smell of hamburgers came at him in strong waves.

The door opened when he tried it. He stepped into a large, dark room with more fish netting everywhere along the walls. A guy behind a tiki bar glanced up at him. The guy looked to be in his mid-twenties, tall and thin. He had a shaggy haircut with a weedy-looking beard. He wore a black T-shirt with a bull's-eye in the center that said AIM TASER HERE. Not a very funny joke. He had been stacking glasses on the shelves behind him, because he turned back to that job while Barn took a moment to let his eyes adjust.

"We're not open for another fifteen minutes," the guy said over his shoulder. "We open at one."

Barn checked his phone. It was 12:59.

"Oh, well, it's almost one."

"Fifteen minutes," the guy repeated. "The chef's just getting things started."

"Do you mind if I take a seat over here?" Barn said,

pointing to a circular settee. "The sun . . ."

"I don't mind if you take a seat in fifteen minutes, pal. That's the best I can do."

Barn nodded.

People were weird, he decided.

He went outside and waited ten minutes. Two cars arrived. Both emptied out right into the restaurant. The passengers didn't come out again, so Barn assumed they had been seated. Usually people treated adults with more courtesy than they treated kids. That was the way of the world.

He pushed through the door again.

The guy with the taser shirt nodded to him.

"Now we're open."

Barn was hungry enough that he didn't care about the guy's rudeness. He slid into the cranberry-colored settee he had noticed before. The taser guy told him to take a one-top, not a whole booth. He had a nasal voice, a honk, really.

Barn took a tiny corner table by the canal side of the restaurant. It had a good window on the water. He had never been in a sit-down restaurant by himself, but he had gone enough with his mom and Aunt Jupiter to know what to expect. All he wanted was a hamburger and fries. He checked his phone while he waited for the waiter, or the taser guy, or whoever was supposed to take his order. Nothing new dinged up on the phone except a blast from the AQUATARIUM, Lucas's store, offering discounts on filters and aquarium packages. The prices looked pretty good.

He went to the Global Shark Attack File. There was an attack on a woman swimming in Fort Lauderdale. He read the details. It sounded like a tiger shark attack. It had hit and gone off, then had circled for a time before two people in a skiff had pulled the woman into their boat. She had been training for a triathlon. She was expected to survive.

"So what do you want there, sport?" the taser guy asked.

He had a pad of paper in his hand to take Barn's order. Barn noticed a name tag on the taser guy's shirt. Brett. Two *t*'s.

"A hamburger and French fries, please."

Brett nodded. He wrote down the order.

"To drink?"

"Water, please."

"Anything else?"

Barn shook his head. Brett kept writing on his order pad.

It took him a long time to write out a simple order, Barn thought.

"What are you, on some kind of vacation or something?" Brett asked, finally folding the order book back.

"Yes, midwinter vacation."

"Feels like nobody ever goes to school anymore," Brett said, and left.

Barn was considering how much he disliked the guy when his phone buzzed. It was Jessup. Barn took the call and said hello.

"Might be onto something with that," Jessup said, first thing. "It's worth thinking about. Where in the world did you learn about the ampullae of Lorenzini?"

"I don't know. I read about them."

"I wish the students I had when I taught college biology bothered to read about such things," Jessup said with his long, heavy drawl. "I'd still be teaching if they did. I promise you."

"It's probably a long shot. Food is the more likely solution."

"You're right about that. But it could be a combination. It's a good suggestion."

Barn didn't know what to add. He pictured Jessup standing and talking into the phone, maybe wearing pajamas. Maybe wearing his machete strapped to his leg even in his pajamas. That image made Barn smile.

"Where are you now?" asked Jessup.

Barn told him.

"I know that place. I'll be in touch later. We may take a boat ride to check on a nesting site, but we'll be outside the Apple Way Canal. Maybe you'd like to come along if we do."

"I sure would."

"I have a few other things to sort out today, but if we go, I'll contact you, okay?"

"Okay."

Jessup hung up. Barn did, too. He was starving. He put his napkin on his lap. Then he checked the Grapefruit League results. The Red Sox had lost two to the Twins. Pitching gave up a ton of hits.

"Burger, fries," Brett said, sliding the plate to Barn. "There you go."

"And a glass of water, please."

"We'll have to charge you."

"For water?"

The guy nodded.

"Okay, I guess."

"You guess?"

"It just seems like water might be free."

"Air is free, buddy. People pay for water around here."

Barn nodded. Aunt Jupiter always said don't fight with people who have disagreeable personalities. It was like throwing gasoline on a fire. Besides, Barn was a kid and he knew kids didn't have much pushback against adults.

Brett left. Barn put ketchup on everything, then ate the food faster than he should have. But he couldn't help it. It was decent. Not great, not bad, but decent. The chef had put a slice of avocado on the side and that was the best part of the meal. The freshest. His mom would have said eat more avocado, skip the burger.

Barn had almost finished when he heard a loud *thwaaaaccccckkkkk* from outside the restaurant. The whole place stopped moving. Probably ten people paused in whatever they were doing and looked around. Two men stood up, both with napkins in their hands, and walked toward the large window fronting the canal. Barn went there, too.

It was Ben Paio, the argumentative guy from the night before, the one who wanted to dynamite the canal. He stood in a sixteen-foot motorboat, an M-80 in his hand. He had a lighter in his other hand, and as Barn watched, Ben lit the fuse and tossed the huge firecracker into the water behind the boat. Barn counted to three, then the charge detonated. It made a big, compressive *thummmmmpppppp*. A kid driving the boat yelled in happiness. Ben smiled, too. Water sprayed up to follow the explosion and then the bed of canal water beneath it rocked like mad back and forth. The motorboat putted slowly downstream. When they were thirty yards downstream, Ben threw another M-80 into the water. Barn watched as the water exploded.

"Local entertainment," Brett said in a loud voice. "That's all for today."

But it wasn't.

Because Barn saw two things he hadn't noticed before. The first thing was a large empty lot across from the restaurant. Around twenty solar panels stood glimmering in the midday sun. Barn watched the sun reflecting off the surfaces. They made heat waves in the air.

And the other thing Barn saw was a kitchen worker from

the Restaurant Restaurant heave a bucket full of slop into the water below. The worker pounded the plastic bucket against the side of the canal to get the last drops out, then turned the bucket over, sat on it, and pulled out a mango from his apron pocket. He bit into the mango and slipped a hand under his chin to deflect the juice spilling out of the fruit.

Below him, Barn imagined, the water had begun to swirl.

21

When he finished, Barn paid the bill and took his time leaving. He didn't want to spend another minute in the Restaurant Restaurant, but he had taken an interest in its food disposal. The situation seemed perfectly ripe: a bed of solar panels and a food source on opposite sides of the canal. That didn't mean the sharks came up and waited around just for those moments when the slop came hurtling down to them, but it all fit together. The sharks had found a spot where they would find food regularly. The electric impulses might have stimulated them. Given the lack of any other observable causes along the canal, the combination of the solar panels and the food deliveries made the most sense.

He texted Finn and Margaret when he made it out to his Swagtron.

Found a place with a restaurant and solar panels.

Then he erased the message. He hadn't explained the possible connection about the solar panels to Finn and Margaret. He composed a second text.

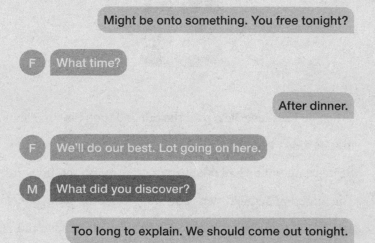

Barn climbed on his Swagtron and drove back to his house. He felt excited, but tired. His mom wasn't home. He took some lemonade from the refrigerator and sat in the quiet to drink it. He deliberately left his phone alone. He didn't read or think about any projects. He simply sat in the quiet at the kitchen table and enjoyed a glass of lemonade.

When he finished his lemonade he went into his bedroom and spent some time working on his aquariums. That was another good way to calm himself. Watching the miniature sharks, listening to the gentle bubbling from the filter, always soothed him. He would never have said it aloud to anyone, but when the light from aquariums shone just right, and when the fish seemed contented and calm, he sometimes felt like a fish himself. Goofy, he knew. But that's the way it sometimes felt.

He had just finished working on his last aquarium when he heard his mom push in through the kitchen door.

"Barn, honey, are you here?"

"In here, Mom."

She came to his room and stopped in the doorway. She wore her yoga clothes. She had gone to a practice with Holly.

"Jessup Sabine is outside," she said. "Do you have plans? Something about a boat?"

"Really? He didn't honk or anything. I didn't know he was out there."

"We talked for a few minutes. He arrived right as I was pulling up."

Barn looked at his mom. She blushed. He got most of his red coloring from his dad, but his mom was fair, too, and when she blushed she turned into a strawberry Popsicle. Barn didn't know what to say. It was just weird.

"Does he want me to . . ."

"Yes, yes, get moving. He's going to take a boat up near the canal, I guess. Something bird related. He told me about the nose pore things . . ."

"Ampullae of Lorenzini."

She looked at him and her brow furrowed. Not out of annoyance, but out of curiosity.

"How do you know these things, Barn?"

Barn shrugged. He had started throwing things into a small backpack. Whatever calmness he felt before had been replaced by excitement.

"I'm trusting you two," his mom said. "Please don't put yourself in danger."

"What two?"

"You and Jessup."

Jessup, Barn wondered. His mom called Jessup Sabine by his first name like you would call anyone else. Then again, what *would* she call him?

174

"We'll be okay, Mom."

"Just don't be reckless. And also, I signed a waiver form for you with Jessup. You are officially an intern with Florida Fish and Game. He needed you to sign that before he could take you out on the boat."

"Thanks, Mom. That's awesome."

He finished shoving things in his backpack.

"You have a sweater?"

"A sweatshirt."

"Sunblock?"

He nodded.

"Did you eat lunch?"

"Yes. I had a hamburger."

"Okay, then. Don't be out too late. I can't believe I am sending you off with a man who has a machete tied to his leg."

"A half machete, Mom."

"Whatever. It's a big knife."

She wouldn't let him pass until he hugged her. She kissed his cheek, then stepped to one side. He hurried out the front door and went to the driver's side window.

"Hi, Dr. Sabine," he said.

"Just call me Jessup. Thought we'd run out to the bay and check things out. How does that sound?"

"Sounds great."

"Hop in, Barn. Your mom told you she signed you up as an intern?"

"Yes."

"Okay, come on, then."

He scrambled around the back and climbed in the passenger side. Jessup didn't have a possum on the floor today. In fact, the van looked recently vacuumed. Barn swung his backpack down between his legs.

"Hope you don't mind country music," Jessup said, turning on the van's ignition.

Then he slipped the van into reverse and they headed out.

22

The boat was cool. It was a Florida Fish and Game patrol boat, a 2020 Sea Born, blue and white, with a 107-inch beam and maybe twenty-four feet in length. It was docked at a tiny boat launch six miles from Apple Way Canal at a swampy piece of land that Jessup said belonged to the state. Kelly, Jessup's intern from the University of Florida, was already on the boat when they arrived. She waved when they pulled in.

"Kelly, this is Barn. Barn, Kelly Bean. She's studying rays and skates over at the University of Florida."

Barn had seen her at Jessup's office before, but he hadn't been introduced formally. Now he was. He shook Kelly's hand. She wore the biggest-brimmed baseball hat he had ever seen. It looked like an enormous bird beak. She was short and nimble, with black hair and a round face. Barn liked her immediately.

"And you're the shark expert," Kelly said, handing out life jackets. "Jessup told me about you."

"Not an expert," Barn said, swinging into his life jacket. "Far from it."

"Don't let him kid you, Kelly. He knows sharks. Sharks and rays are related, so you two are almost like cousins."

All this time Jessup had been untying ropes and getting the boat ready. He and Kelly had obviously worked together before, because she went to the steering wheel while he pushed the boat away from the dock. He hopped on at the last moment and as soon as he was aboard, she goosed the engines.

This is amazing, Barn thought.

He wanted to yell, or make some sort of shout, but that would have been uncool. Instead he stepped up under the cuddy canopy and held on as Kelly navigated the shallow water in the swamp.

"Lot of gators in here," Jessup said. "Keep an eye out, you'll see them."

"Good tarpon fishing, too," Kelly shouted over the engine sounds. "You a fisherman, Barn?"

"Not so much."

"Well, I love to go for bonefish, but mostly I go to the flats to study rays. They love the flats, my rays."

"Bend her around to the west," Jessup said, pointing with his prosthetic arm, then turned to Barn. "I thought we'd check out the entrance to the canal. Just see if there's anything we can notice. We have some other projects out that way, too. We won't be out long."

Barn nodded. He was happy to go anywhere in the boat.

"We've seen a snail kite nest, we think," Jessup said, continuing. "It's on the endangered species list, so we want to make sure. Usually they stick to the Everglades, but maybe they've ranged over here. Hard to say. Apple snails have come in and displaced the native varieties, so the snail kites are walking a thin line."

"There's a gator right there," Kelly cut into the conversation. "You see him, Barn? Up on the bank there. Is that Old Froggy, Jessup?"

"Looks like him," Jessup agreed. "Big male who makes a heck of a racket bellowing during mating season. He's been around here for a couple years. I can't quite tell the way he's back in the rushes. Looks like him, though."

Barn felt as if he had died and gone to heaven. Trying to take everything in at once, he knew his eyes were as big as onions. He had always known that some people somewhere studied animals and engaged them for a profession, but he had never quite understood it as he understood it now, standing on the boat. It was awesome. The sun had started to soften and edge toward the western horizon and everything had a soft, quiet air. He moved to the starboard side of the boat and looked at the shoreline. Everything here was liquid. Even the land seemed to float on water. Barn noted a huge grove of mangroves. The roots arched and twined everywhere, dipping into the water like so many wooden straws. Mangroves served as nursery grounds for a dozen species of fish, Barn knew. He had never seen it quite as clearly, however, as he did now.

Jessup shouted something and immediately afterward Kelly cut the engines. The boat continued forward, drifting, its wake passing out in a V to both sides.

"That's the bay," Jessup said, coming to stand next to Barn. "The beginning of it, anyway. You follow that up and you'll come to three canals that fork off it. Apple Way is the northernmost branch."

"Any reports of sharks in the other two?" Barn asked.

"Nothing special. Just regular sea life. The Apple Way Canal is deeper than the other two. That might have something to do with it."

"Do you think the solar panels I told you about might attract them?"

Jessup shrugged.

"Hard to say," he said. "Could be. It's as good a working theory as any. Kelly, did you hear what Barn found up the canal? Solar array right across the canal from the Restaurant Restaurant. He said the kitchen help throws food into the canal."

"We should cite them for that," Kelly said. "That's bad practice."

"That could be enough to attract sharks. Just the food, I mean," Jessup said. "Plus an electric charge bleeding into the water . . . that's a dinner bell."

"Pull one thread and others follow," Kelly said. "Nice

job, Barn. That's at least a place to start. Violations like that can cause all sorts of unintended consequences."

"We don't have time today, but we could go up there tomorrow," Jessup said. "It's almost quitting time."

Kelly held an enormous pair of binoculars against her eyes. She scanned the tree line, looking, Barn supposed, for the snail kite's nest. The boat drifted more and nudged against a half-submerged log. For a second Barn thought the log was a gator, but it was merely a log.

"See anything?" Jessup asked Kelly.

She shook her head.

"Let's go up to the canal head and see what's there. We don't have time to do the whole trip, but we can look at the entrance. How does that sound to you two?"

That was the plan. Barn sat on the gunwale and took in the light and air as they made their way toward the canal entrance. He would never have been able to find it on his own, and even Jessup had to look at the GPS screen beside Kelly. Finally they got it right. Kelly touched the engines hard and the boat slowly lifted into a hydroplane. They skimmed the surface like a stone touching water every third jump.

23

Barn waited in the shadows. It was early evening still, just after dinner, and Finn and Margaret had texted they were on their way. The sun hadn't quite set completely, but the shadows from the Restaurant Restaurant and from the trees near the canal had softened and blended into the evening dimness. A few bats whisked around above him and crickets had begun to call. A quarter moon sat on the eastern horizon.

It felt exciting to be out, to be watching, to be checking the business for illegal dumping. Barn had a notion that the restaurant threw a bunch more of its food scraps into the water than anyone knew. If it did, if he could link the garbage to the uptick in the presence of sharks in the canal, then Jessup would know what to do about it. As it stood, though, it was an unproven hypothesis. One bucket—whatever he had seen the kitchen worker do that afternoon—did not prove anything. One bucket did not make his case.

He heard Finn make a loon call.

It was a call they both used to locate each other. You made it by cupping your hands together, then blowing between your thumbs on the hollow your hands created. It made a high, warbling sound.

Barn put his lips to his thumbs and returned the loon call.

A second later Finn and Margaret pulled into the Restaurant Restaurant driveway.

"Over here," Barn whispered.

It felt funny whispering. He couldn't tell for certain if they truly needed to be stealthy. Maybe so. It was amusing, anyway.

"Hi, Barn," Margaret said, climbing off her bike.

Barn saw she had fixed a small aftermarket engine to her bike. It made him smile.

"Did you make your bike . . ."

"Electric motor. Same as yours, I think."

"I rigged it up," Finn said, snapping up his Dead Days Pintail Longboard. "It goes hard."

"That's cool," Barn said. "Now we can move faster if we have to."

They retreated a little farther into the shadows. Once they had positioned themselves out of sight of the restaurant, Barn explained what he had seen, what he suspected. He told them about the array of solar panels across the canal. That caught Finn's interest.

"If they run any sort of power line underwater from the solar panels to the restaurant, then it's bound to have a discharge and the sharks will lock onto that."

"Along with the food from the kitchen," Margaret said, nodding. "It makes sense."

"Maybe. I told Jessup about it and he said it's a promising lead, but not definite. He's going to come up and talk to the owner tomorrow. We need to see what they actually throw in the canal. I don't want Jessup coming up here if I got something wrong. We need to confirm what's going on."

"Let me use your Swagtron and I'll go over and check out the solar panels," Finn said. "I'll see if I can detect anything. You guys stay here and watch the kitchen."

It was a good plan, but Barn felt his heart go a little funny knowing he would be left alone with Margaret. He tried to think of some flaw in Finn's plan, but he couldn't come up with anything.

"Okay, but don't be too long," he whispered, and pointed. "The bridge is right up there."

Finn nodded. He set his longboard against a tree, threw his leg over the bar of the Swagtron, and pedaled off. A second later Barn heard the engine turn on.

"I've always wanted to do a stakeout," Margaret said, giggling a little. "It's so cool. I even wore dark clothes on purpose."

She had on a black hoodie and black jeans. She looked cool.

"Well, it might not amount to much," he admitted.

"But it could. And it's fun to sneak around, anyway. I used to love playing hide-and-seek and games like that."

"Are you okay being out this late?"

"It's not that late. My parents aren't exactly dialed in right now. They're splitting up. That's what I was doing in Fort Lauderdale today. Seeing them."

"I'm sorry. I wondered if it was something like that."

She blew air past her bottom lip.

"I hate it all, but I guess it's what they have to do. That's why I'm staying with Finn's folks. They're friends of my parents."

Barn nodded. He knew that her parents were friends with Finn's parents, but he hadn't known *why* she had been staying with Finn. And Finn—because he was the best kind of friend—had kept her secret because that's what Finn did.

"Sorry."

"My dad's moving over to Fort Lauderdale. I'll stay here with my mom. I went over to see his place. It's nice. It looks out on the Intracoastal Waterway. It has a pool. I guess he can play golf if he wants to."

"Well, that's good," Barn said, because he wasn't sure what else to say.

"You know, you go along and you think everything is one way, but it's not what you think. What anyone thinks. Life can change fast."

Barn nodded. His dad had died fast. His dad had been alive one minute, dead the next. Yes, things could change fast.

He looked over at Margaret. He wanted to say something good, something consoling, but she smiled a soft, wan smile. Then she pointed to the back deck of the restaurant.

"There," she whispered.

He followed her line of sight. It was Brett, the waiter who had been rude to him when he had lunch earlier in the day. Brett pulled a large wheeled garbage can—the big plastic kind, one nearly as tall as a pony—behind him onto the flat boards of the deck. Two other guys, both wearing kitchen whites, came out with him. A woman from inside the dining area stepped outside, too. Brett opened the lid of the garbage can and dug a long-handled stockpot into the contents. He shook the pot, and the refuse—food scraps, Barn guessed—scattered on the surface of the water. It looked like rain. A second later, the woman laughed in a loud, happy voice. One of the guys in kitchen whites said, "Oh, man!"

They were all looking down at the water below the deck.

They were feeding the sharks.

Barn couldn't see the water directly, but it seemed obvious that's what they were doing. Brett dug pot after pot out of the larger garbage vat and chucked it down on the canal. Sometimes the woman yelled, sometimes one of the kitchen guys. After each pot full of swill, Brett grinned and made a motion that said, *See, I told you.* It seemed pretty clear it was a thing they did nightly. It got rid of the restaurant waste and it gave them a little show at the end of their shift. Barn doubted they had ever made the connection to the death of Robby White.

"You were right, Barn," Margaret whispered. "They're feeding them."

"That's such a bad idea. That's crazy."

"But you were right."

"It still doesn't mean they're responsible for Robby White's death."

"No, I know, but it's a bad situation, isn't it?"

"It's a bad situation. Really bad."

Finn came back at that moment. He parked the Swagtron and hustled over to squat beside them.

"It's definitely giving the restaurant a feed. The solar panels. They have a main cable going right into the water across from the deck there."

"They're feeding the sharks, too," Margaret said.

"No way," Finn said.

For a few minutes they simply watched. Barn counted seventeen ladles of food. Seventeen ladles was a lot of food. By the time Brett got to the last few, he simply threw things in as fast as he could. It was dark now and the viewing was likely not great.

The kitchen guys went back inside. Brett wheeled the garbage can back next to the restaurant. Barn didn't see the woman disappear, but she was no longer there. He guessed the darkness had obscured her departure.

"What do we do?" whispered Margaret.

"I want to see what they were looking at," Barn said.

"So do I," Finn said.

"Shouldn't we just tell Jessup?" Margaret wondered.

"We will. But I want to know what I'm telling him."

"They can't stop us from looking," Finn said. "They have a public business."

"They won't like it, though," Margaret warned them. "People can be touchy when you catch them doing something wrong."

Barn stood. His friends stood beside him.

"Let it get a little darker," he said. "Maybe they won't even see us."

"This is so cool," Margaret said.

"She wore black so she would blend in," Finn said.

"I know," Barn said. "She told me."

24

Barn watched the last car pull out of the parking lot. He wasn't sure, but he thought it belonged to Brett. Maybe Brett was the owner. It seemed like it to Barn.

"Ready?" Barn whispered.

"We don't need to whisper, do we?" Finn asked, standing and stepping into the light of the parking lot. "They're gone."

"It's still good to be careful," Margaret said. "You never know."

"If anyone comes, scatter and stay in the shadows," Barn said, joining Finn in the light. Margaret came right behind him. "They probably won't bother chasing kids."

"How are we going to test this?" Finn asked.

"Same way they did," Barn said. "There's probably some food left in that can."

"Is this illegal? I kind of hope it's illegal," Margaret said.

"You're a regular cat burglar," Finn said. "Let's do this."

Barn noticed the moon had gone behind a cloud. It was dark. A single floodlight on the corner of the building shone down onto the parking lot. Behind the restaurant the deck looked black and still. Finn made them wait while he looked for cameras. He found one located above the front door, hidden under a fake fishing net. It monitored the lot and the front entrance.

"I think we're okay," Finn said, skirting around to look. "The deck might have an automated light system. A motion sensor."

"We'll have to risk it," said Margaret.

"We have to make it fast," Barn said. "Just on and off. We probably already know what we're going to see."

"Let me try this first," Finn said.

He bent down and picked up a handful of gravel and tossed it onto the deck. It made a loud noise, but no light came on and that was a good sign, Barn figured. Barn asked if Finn had brought a flashlight. Finn looked at him and made a face that meant: *Are you joking?* Barn had a flashlight on his phone, but he didn't exactly want to be holding it over a large body of water that could possibly contain sharks. Of course Finn had a flashlight, Barn realized. If it ran on electricity, Finn usually had it.

Finn swung off his backpack and pulled out a headlamp. He put it on and moved toward the two wooden steps up to the deck. Barn followed him and when Finn glanced at the garbage can and nodded to indicate that was it, Barn stepped quickly to the container and began pulling it to the edge of the deck.

It was quiet. Barn heard the hum generated by the batteries charged by the solar panels. A quiet hum. The grind of the garbage can wheels was the loudest thing around.

"Do me a favor," Barn said to Finn. "Look down in the garbage can, and when I throw the food, move the light so we can see the surface. Okay?"

"Okay."

"Margaret, if you don't mind, you could throw stuff, too."

"How do we get it out?"

"I guess with our hands."

Barn hadn't gone that far in his thinking, but that was the best solution. He flipped back the lid of the garbage can and waited while Finn ran his light around the content. Gross. Major gross. Barn didn't want to look too carefully at what he needed to pluck from the interior. Chicken parts, he saw. And something like a ham, shaved in half, with a few tooth-picks sticking out of it. To his surprise, Margaret stuck her hands in first. She grabbed the ham and didn't show any signs of gross-out.

"Ready?" she whispered.

Barn grabbed a few pieces of chicken. He held them above his head, ready to throw. Finn's light beam passed from Margaret's hand to Barn's hand.

"On three," Barn said. "Finn, as soon as we throw it, look down at the surface so we can see what happens. You ready?"

"Ready," Finn said.

"One, two . . ."

Before he could throw the chicken parts, Barn heard the door to the restaurant open. A second later he heard the jingle of a dog's collar, and a low, horrible growl.

At the same time he heard someone shout, "Get them!"

The dog's claws made a grating sound as it came across the gravel of the walkway and then a clicking, rapid sound on the boards of the deck. Barn watched Finn and Margaret scatter. He ducked behind the garbage can, using it to fend off the dog.

But the dog was too quick.

It was a small dog, compact and rust-colored, maybe an Australian cattle dog. It lunged at Barn as soon as it discovered him behind the garbage can. Barn shoved the can at the dog, but the dog was too quick and nimble. It shot around the edge of the garbage can, its lips curled back, its teeth flashing forward for a bite. Barn swung the garbage can at the dog, but in swinging it he lost his balance.

And in that instant he felt his foot miss its support.

He had been too near the edge and the lunging dog threw off his balance. He made a quick, terrified grab for the garbage can, but like a haunted coffin stood up on its end, the plastic can simply followed him. Everything went to slow motion, and he saw Margaret and Finn duck and dart away. They ran toward the parking lot side of the restaurant and leaped off the deck steps. But Barn continued to grab at the garbage can, the plastic coffin. It did not respond but instead skidded more as his need for it grew.

He heard someone groan, someone nearby. Only in his fifth heartbeat did he realize he had made the sound.

And on his sixth heartbeat, and on the heartbeat that removed him from the earth, he realized he was falling into the black water that waited below.

25

Barn hit the water hard.

His wind chugged out of his body and he felt something large and hollow hit his trailing foot. The garbage can made a loud whacking noise as it struck the water and struck his foot. Barn held up his hands, trying to fend off the rest of its weight.

The water shocked him.

It took his breath and he felt himself growing panicked like a wild seed caught in the wind. *No, no, no, no*, his mind repeated over and over and over.

He felt something move past him, something fast and rough, and he did not doubt that he had been bumped by a bull shark. They had been trained to eat whatever was thrown into the canal. Now he was in the canal. Now he was food.

"Barn," Finn called.

They had come back.

"Swim to the ladder!" Margaret almost screamed.

What ladder, Barn wondered.

Someone shouted at the dog, too. He heard that. But before he could process that . . .

. . . something hit his leg . . .

. . . hard.

His knee. The force of the blow swung his leg back in his hip joint and he wondered if he had been bitten. Often people didn't know when they were bitten. Usually they went shock-y and couldn't remember how the attack had occurred until later. He didn't doubt he had been grazed by a shark, with teeth or without. Blood would not show up easily on the dark canal surface.

"Over there, over there, over there," Margaret yelled.

It was good of her to help, but he didn't know where *over there* was.

"Downstream, ten yards," Finn said.

That was more help.

Then Barn had a good idea.

He climbed onto the garbage can. It wasn't easy and the can wasn't fully afloat, but at least it was partially out of the water. Somehow it had caught air on its way down and had turned upside down. Now it bobbed like a bottle in the canal, and Barn threw his body across it and began paddling like crazy toward the ladder.

"Go, go, go, go," Margaret screamed.

Above him, Barn heard people yelling. He sent his senses down to his leg, wondering if he had been bitten. If the shark got an artery he would die. But he still didn't know if he had been bitten, couldn't see in the darkness, and he clung to the garbage can and kept his body pressed close to it. Now, he hoped, the ampullae of Lorenzini worked in his favor, because the sharks might not detect electrical impulses from him if he could be confused with the garbage can.

That's what he thought, anyway. He didn't know if it made sense.

More yelling and screaming on the deck. Dog barks. Lights on. Barn didn't want the light. In the light he might see his leg, the true condition, and he wasn't sure he wanted to see that. While he thought about the light, something else slammed against the garbage can. The plastic quivered with the impact and Barn understood the force of an attack. It was like being hit by a bat as well as being bitten. The garbage can jerked up once, then shrugged down in the water and bobbed back up again.

Barn saw the ladder. It was a typical marine ladder screwed into the piers of the canal walls. It was only five feet away, but Barn understood he would have to leave the relative safety of the garbage can to make it to the ladder. The can dragged too far down; its draw was too much for the shallow bank near the canal wall. Barn would have to surge off the garbage can and stretch out, exposing his ribs, his body, his everything, to the underwater swirls of the sharks.

"Look out, Barn, look out!" Finn yelled.

Look out for what? Barn wanted to answer in frustration. Everything danced and moved and churned. He could barely tell one thing from another. Maybe, he considered, he was losing consciousness.

He took a breath and shoved off the garbage can.

He swam as fast and as hard as he could toward the

ladder. His foot hit something below him and he didn't think it was a shark. It could have been anything under the water, anything solid, and he kicked past it, not sure what reports his body sent back to his brain, not sure of anything.

He felt his body lifted out of the water.

Lifted!

It took him an instant to realize a bull shark had passed directly beneath him. A huge bull shark. Its body had pushed him up and out of the water for one heartbeat, then he had splashed down behind the shark. In the same moment his hand found the metal rung of the ladder. He pulled up, clawing, his feet digging at the wall of the canal. He yanked himself higher on the ladder and at last he felt himself returned to air, not water. He glanced down quickly to see if his leg remained with his body.

It was there.

Nothing had been removed.

Realizing he had escaped, he almost fell back into the water out of relief. That was nutty, but he felt such joy and exhilaration that his fingers almost unclasped themselves. Luckily, he caught himself. He glanced down again to check his leg and that's when he saw the shark swim by.

It was the shark that had lifted him. It was ten feet at least, and heavy. A surge of water moved in front of it. When Barn looked down, the shark looked up. For an electric moment their eyes met. Then the shark disappeared. The water stilled. The garbage can simply bobbed its way calmly downstream on the lowering tide.

26

Barn refused to let go of the ladder.

He refused help from Finn and Margaret and he even refused the police officer who bent down and leaned over and spoke to him calmly.

"It's okay, it's okay, it's okay," the officer said repeatedly.

It was okay, Barn knew, because he held tight to the ladder.

Sharks swam below.

"Come on up," the police officer said. "No one's going to hurt you. You're okay."

Thinking about danger was one thing, Barn realized. Living in danger was another.

Either way, he didn't want to let go of the ladder.

"Just come up one rung," the officer said. "Your mom is on her way. Everything is going to be all right."

Barn stared at the officer. He was a middle-aged guy with a crew cut. He wore a tan uniform shirt and dark trousers. He had a thick belt around his waist. Barn saw the man's holster and sidearm. The belt made leather creaking sounds.

"You're okay now," the officer said. "You're all right."

Barn didn't know if he should believe the officer. The only thing he knew he should believe was the feel of the metal ladder rung under his hand. That was the only thing he could be certain of in this moment. He believed the officer enough to lift one hand and try for the rung above, but that meant giving over some of his weight to one hand and that hand might slip and that hand might dump him back . . .

. . . in the water.

With the sharks.

Barn closed his eyes and held on to the ladder.

"Come on, son," the officer said. "You've had a shock, no doubt, but up you come. Come on, now. You've made it this far."

Barn shook his head. He wanted to obey the officer, but

the officer didn't know what it was like to be lifted free of the water by a shark. The officer didn't know what it was like to feel a rigid dorsal fin draw a line across your belly.

Then Barn heard a different voice. The officer moved away. In his place, Jessup leaned over the wall.

"Hi, Barn," Jessup said, his voice like a big block of wood. "You had quite a close call."

Barn nodded.

"What you're feeling is shock. Your blood pressure has dropped. You probably feel clammy and light-headed. Your body temperature has dropped, too, I'm guessing. I'm talking to you as one scientist to another. Your body is shutting down the blood supply to nonessential organs and redirecting it to your chest and abdomen. That's why you may feel a tingling in your arms and legs. You have to be careful not to let it get too far. The shock, I mean. You could pass out and you'd be right back in the water. So do you want me to climb down and help you up? Or do you think you can make it?"

Barn nodded.

He didn't know what a nod meant in that moment. But it seemed the thing to do.

"Take deep breaths. Move one hand up and one leg at the

same time. Then again. That's all there is to it. Your body went into survival mode and it's only coming out of it bit by bit. Trust me."

He did trust Jessup. But he had trouble letting go of the ladder rung.

"I'll tell you what," Jessup said. "We could tie a safety harness around you if you think that would ease your mind. How would that be?"

Barn's entire body shivered. It felt like finding a spider on your pillow. You just react.

And in one big breath, he shot up the ladder. He didn't know how or why. He just went up the ladder and came up onto his feet and Jessup pulled him away and steadied him.

"There you go. There you go," Jessup said.

He had his arm around Barn. It felt weird, but good, too.

An EMT team suddenly appeared. Barn slowly realized this had been a *thing*. A lot of people had shown up. Two service vehicles had bright lights that looped around and around the entire scene. One in yellow, one in red. He saw Margaret. She had her knuckle in her mouth, biting it.

"Are you okay?" she asked.

He didn't know the answer to that question.

He looked at her and shrugged. Finn stood beside her.

Then an EMT named Lucy led him to a gurney and made him sit on it. The sheet that covered the slim mattress felt wonderfully dry. Barn shivered again and Lucy tucked a blanket around him. It was over, he realized. He was out of the water. The sharks hadn't killed him after all.

She told him to stretch out on the gurney. He did. Before they could lift him and move him inside, he saw his mom. She tore through the small crowd and fell on him. She hugged him so hard he worried it might break a rib. He figured if she could hug him hard then maybe there wasn't much wrong with him.

"I can just come home," he said to Lucy.

She shook her head.

"You're going to have a checkup. No big deal, but we want to be certain . . ."

"Just take him," Barn heard his mom say. "I'm going with him."

That's what happened. Barn felt himself lifted into the ambulance and a second later his mom climbed in beside him. The light above kept circling and punching holes in the darkness. Barn felt himself getting sleepy. Adrenaline, he knew. His body had gone into fight-or-flight response mode and now, when it was over, he needed sleep.

His mom held his hand. The ambulance driver hit the siren enough to chirp. Not a full siren, just enough to clear people away. Then Barn felt the ambulance start to move at a normal pace. He heard his mother's voice from far away. Sleep crawled over him like an ant going up a dandelion stalk.

EPILOGUE

Barn watched the Red Sox take batting practice. The Sox stood in third place in the Grapefruit League, their record at 4–7. Barn didn't care. The Grapefruit season was one thing and the regular season was another. The Sox had amazing talent. They were predicted to win a hundred games.

He sat in the best seat he had ever had for a game. Jessup Sabine knew a friend who knew a friend who had spring training tickets. He got them for Barn as a recovery present. Everyone gave him recovery presents. Grandpa Lemon sent him a book on sailboats and Aunt Jupiter had made him a huge vat of caramel popcorn. It was a little strange to receive gifts because he hadn't been bitten. His injuries had been psychological, and that, his mom reminded him, could be every bit as serious as physical injuries.

Barn knew his mom was right. Sometimes, sometimes, he felt the sharks lift him up again.

But he shook himself now in the stands and took a breath. It was a perfect day for baseball. Blue skies, white clouds, a gentle breeze that barely lifted the pennants on the foul poles. He sat between Margaret and Finn. He couldn't tell if either of them liked the game. He knew Finn wasn't much of a fan. He wasn't sure about Margaret. Baseball wasn't everybody's thing.

Jessup sat on the other side of his mother.

And that was a little strange. But maybe not. They seemed to laugh a lot.

Jessup had driven Aunt Jupiter to pick up his mother's car the night of the sharks. When he returned, he seemed to be around a good bit.

Barn didn't mind the sun today. That much was different. But after the shark night, he seemed cold down in his bones. He couldn't get warm. Still, he was better off than Brett, who was in all kinds of trouble. The dog, it turned out, had bitten three other people. Brett liked siccing the dog on anyone who came onto the restaurant property after hours. The dog had also bitten a kid at the local playground earlier in the year. Besides the problem with the dog, Brett had been charged with littering, assault, and unlawful disposal of restaurant waste. The Restaurant Restaurant had closed the next day and hadn't reopened. Brett had huge fines to pay.

And the sharks had stopped coming to the restaurant dock. Jessup had stretched a metal net across the canal fifty feet below the restaurant and he had shocked the water above it. They had counted a dozen sharks of varying lengths near the restaurant dock. Jessup had released them below the net. He had also checked the electric cable connecting the solar panels to the restaurant.

"Anyone want a hot dog?" Jessup asked, his head bending forward to see past Barn's mom.

"No thanks," Margaret said.

"I would," Barn said. "Thank you."

"Me, too," Finn said.

Jessup waved for one of the vendors who sold hot dogs out of a heated box he wore on a strap around his neck. The vendor opened his box and grabbed out four dogs.

"What's in a hot dog?" Margaret whispered to Barn.

She leaned close. Her breath caught in his ear.

"Unicorn meat," he said. "You should try one."

Before she could answer, a Sox player fouled a ball right at them. The ball drifted into the sun and then disappeared on its flight down to the seats. It landed five or six rows over toward home plate. Barn watched the ball bounce up and arc back toward the field. For just an instant, he felt the surge of the shark lift under his body. It had left an abrasion on his calf. He didn't blame the sharks. Millions of years had proved them well designed. He still loved them. He could not close his eyes without picturing them under him, dark gray forms swirling on a black, black night.

CAN'T GET ENOUGH
SHARKS?!?

Here's a sneak preview of
Dragged From Under #2:
The Great White Shark!

"You realize we're the only ones out here, right?" Jimmy said to Dimitri when he paddled up beside him. More than anything else about surfing, Jimmy liked sitting next to his brother and talking.

"So what? We have the place to ourselves."

"That's because the waves suck and it's freezing."

"You surf when you can, my young friend. Learn from your older brother."

Dimitri smiled. He always smiled. He had, Jimmy knew, a sunny disposition. And that could drive you crazy sometimes.

"Do you know you look ridiculous in your wet suit?" Jimmy asked.

Because he did. Dimitri looked like a black, cheerful frog.

"I am one with the sea," Dimitri said. Then he laid down on his board and began paddling hard. "Here comes one."

Jimmy watched him. It was strange to be beyond the break. Jimmy always found it strange. Out beyond the break, anyone paddling for a wave disappeared temporarily, then rose up and suddenly appeared gliding along the water surface. Pretty remarkable, really. Jimmy watched Dimitri until his brother fell off the wave. Then he was alone.

He looked out at the horizon. Far out, misty in the morning fog, he saw a tanker sliding by on its way south. A few clouds tucked close to the horizon, blending with the sea. He could not hear a thing this far out except the gentle wash of the water when it rubbed against the sand of the beach. He smiled.

Dimitri had been right to get him out of bed on such a morning. On any morning, really.

He shook himself. His sleepiness gave way to attention. He could surf. He was a good surfer. That's what he told himself. When it came to bats, balls, and balance, he had skills. Mad skills. He counted three swells, all too puny to try for, but then he saw a good one rolling toward him. It built and piled on itself until he could sense the water's forward momentum.

Okay, he whispered.

Sometimes he whispered to himself. He always had. It steadied him.

He stretched out on the board and dug his hands into the water. He maneuvered his board into position, paddling until he was an arrow on the bow-string of the wave. Now, at last, he felt somewhat warmer. He felt his pecs stretch with the burden of paddling. He kicked softly with his feet, using them as rudders, his breath coming in short, quick pants. Although Dimitri meant it as a joke, Jimmy *did* feel one with the sea. Ridiculous, he told himself. He was turning into a nerd like his brother.

Then something hard and as explosive as Thor's hammer hit him from below.

He flew into the air.

He flew three feet into the air and when he came down the lower half of his body dunked into the water while he grabbed for the board with his arms.

What the . . . , he thought.

If what he felt could be called thought.

He looked around, scared suddenly, and tried to climb back onto the board. In the next instant, however, something fierce and horrible grabbed his leg. He tried to yank it away, but he had nothing to grasp except the board. The board flipped over. It skittered across the surface of the water and then jerked to a stop against the tether.

Something violet and red began spreading around him. A few gulls ducked down and circled close. And then he saw a huge black fin cut the water next to him.

"Shark!" he screamed.

ABOUT THE AUTHOR

Joseph Monninger lives in New Hampshire. His work has appeared in *American Heritage, Scientific American, Reader's Digest, Glamour, Story, Fiction, Sports Illustrated, Boston Globe,* and *Ellery Queen,* among other publications. His young adult novel, *Baby,* was named one of the top ten novels of 2008 by YALSA. He has appeared on the *Today Show* and has written columns for several New Hampshire newspapers. He has been a licensed New Hampshire fishing guide and his family ran a sled dog team for several years in the New England Sled Dog Club.